Mississippi Gumbo

*A Collection of Tales Of
South Mississippi and a Potpourri of
Other Mississippi Writings*

By

Robert E. Jones

© 2003 by Robert E. Jones. All rights reserved.

No part of this book may be reproduced, stored in a retrieval system, or transmitted by any means, electronic, mechanical, photocopying, recording, or otherwise, without written permission from the author.

ISBN: 978-1-4107-8901-3 (sc)
ISBN: 978-1-4107-8902-0 (hc)
ISBN: 978-1-4107-8900-6 (e)

Print information available on the last page.

This book is printed on acid free paper.

1stBooks - rev. 10/10/03

TABLE OF CONTENTS

Colonel Collins, The Great Scot 1

Grierson's Raid 61

The Hobo Heroes 65

Sweet Pea To The Rescue 75

Sam Jones, What Are You Doing Here? 83

The Homecoming 111

Trimble's Barbershop 117

The Sauer Story 123

The Outlaw, The Sheriff And The Governor 131

The Last Legal Hanging In Lincoln County 159

Home Town Lynchings 165

The American Do Nuthin Party Convention 173

Great Things To Ponder 179

The Tragedy Of Peggy O'neal 185

Conversation With An Alien 195

A Hand To Remember 203

A Clown Or A Witch? 209

The Senator Goes To Nashville 211

My Friend Charlie 217

Judgment Day 223

AUTHOR'S NOTES

This book is a potpourri of writings, mostly stories of Mississippi based events, but a smattering of poetry and other things. The longer pieces are biographical and historical; the shorter ones range from college escapades to imaginary conversations, to a game of bridge, a sentimental homecoming of a wayward daughter, a silly musical melodramatic skit, and a one-act farce based on actual events in my family.

I hope the reader will enjoy the variety of themes and perhaps have occasion to suppress a laugh or even a tear.

The play "Sam Jones, What Are You Doing Here?" is an account of events that occurred in the old Jones house on Railroad Avenue in Brookhaven just after World War II. Times and attitudes then in the little Mississippi town were, like the Jones home, in the Victorian style, changed only slightly by the war, and strongly influenced by urgent teetotal Baptist preaching.

"The Outlaw, The Sheriff and The Governor" is the true account of events in southern Lawrence County, Mississippi, near the Oakvale Community in the late 1880's to 1900. The events were first brought to my attention by my uncle, Sam Jones, whose mother was raised by two of the characters in the story, Sheriff Dan Lee and his wife, Matt. Over two years of research uncovered many newspaper accounts of the events; deed and court records furnished more facts.

The original transcript of the testimony in Joe Loftin's first trial was found in the state archives and gave minute details of the murder and other events prior to Joe's conviction. A grandson of Joe in Oklahoma was located and interviewed. The mystery of Joe's release from prison is left for the reader to solve.

"The Hobo Heroes" was printed as an article in Brookhaven's The Daily Leader on November 30, 2000. The story was first told to me by John David Kees who had endeavored tirelessly to get some well-deserved recognition for his old friend, Larry Williamson, for his heroic deeds in the rescue of survivors of the *Juneau* in November 1942.

There are three stories from my old friend Charlie Brennan. One is a wild escapade by him and his college buddy, Bill Peeler, while law students at Cumberland Law School, Lebanon, Tennessee.

Charlie was a wonderfully creative person. Unfortunately, his love affair with the grape had an adverse effect on his life. Bill Peeler became a prominent lawyer in East Tennessee and a political power as majority leader of the state senate.

Also included here is Charlie's epic poem "The Stranger Man" printed with permission of his sister, Marcelle Brennan. I had urged Charlie to write down his many poetic efforts, and he finally did some of them before his death. I modified and edited "The Stranger Man" to improve its flow and meter, but it was entirely Charlie's creation.

Charlie was an avid bridge enthusiast for many years and was instrumental in establishing our town's duplicate bridge club. The "A Hand to Remember" was his story - all true.

The barbershop article appeared in The Daily Leader on October 19, 1998 and is self-explanatory.

"The Homecoming" is based on my mother's true story, semi-tragic at the time of the events. Thankfully, she subsequently married my father and lived happily ever after.

Of course, the "Conversation With an Alien," as you may have suspected, is fiction.

The Col. Charles Glen Collins story is such an amazing saga that it should be expanded into a full-length book. It qualifies as a Mississippi story, since he married the widow of a prominent Brookhaven businessman, an icon of the city, John W. McGrath, whose statute stands in the city's downtown park. When the depression crushed Mrs. McGrath's fortune, she and Collins moved from New Orleans to Brookhaven where he died in 1939. The story of "The Great Scot" ran as ten episodes in The Daily Leader. There may be an occasional repetition from where the episodes overlapped. Please excuse it.

"The American Do Nuthin Party Convention" routine is built around the moderately fictitious character, Senator J. Greyfeather Beauregard, whom I developed over the years for comedy routines. He is a wonderful southern gentleman, but a bit senile. He loves flowery oratory and does not let ethics stand in the way of plagiarizing a good phrase.

"The Tragedy of Peggy O'Neal" farce is a simple and silly little melodrama that gives free range for the actors to have fun and cornball it up to delight the audience. I learned to love the old gay nineties songs listening to my dear talented Aunt Peggy Butterfield Irvin play and sing them enthusiastically when I was a child.

Robert E. Jones
2003

Col. Charles Glen Collins in front of his battalion at Balmoral Castle

COLONEL COLLINS, THE GREAT SCOT

A simple headstone in Brookhaven's Rosehill Cemetery marks the grave of Colonel Charles Glen Collins:

COLLINS

Lili A.
January 12, 1872
May 24, 1944

Charles G.
April 19, 1880
September 21, 1939

Few of the friends who attended the 1939 burial of Colonel Collins knew of the flamboyant background of the Scotsman they honored, or that he was one who was personally acquainted with three English sovereigns, Queen Victoria, Edward VII and George V, as well as Winston Churchill, Sir Herbert Kitchener, the Vanderbilts, J.P. Morgan, Enrico Caruso, William Faulkner and others in the upper social, literary and political circles of London, Paris and New York as well as New Orleans.

The Brookhaven Leader gave him a kind and respectful obituary, noting his remarkable British military service in Africa and in World War I at Gallipoli, as well as his writing a regular column for the local paper.

The New York Times, which was more aware of his national and international prominence, carried a four-paragraph story of his passing, including this paragraph.

> "Colonel Collins, a former lieutenant colonel in the British Army, led a dashing life in this country that made the romantic heroes of fiction seem pale. He was frequently in financial difficulties, married three times, twice to American heiresses, and eventually was taken to India to stand trial for a theft of jewelry, but acquitted."

The first opportunity for people of the mid-South to learn of Colonel Collins was near the end of World War I when he was arrested in New Orleans on two criminal charges by Bombay jewelers for fraud in regard to purchases of expensive jewelry while on a world tour.

<u>The Times Picayune</u> followed his troubles with frequent front-page stories. The Bombay merchants sought to extradite him to India to stand trial for the alleged crime, which at that time in India was a capital offense.

Aware of the grave danger of a Britisher being tried before a jury of native Indians, Collins was understandably determined to fight extradition at all costs. He claimed he had purchased the pearls and jewelry for his fiancé, paying 3000 pounds down and getting credit for the balance of 4500 pounds. However, the funds he was anticipating to make the final payment were to have come from an oil well investment in Houston, Texas.

When that bonanza was slow in coming through, the merchants panicked and filed the charges, influenced by government officials who hoped to use the incident to further whip up resentment against the British in India's fight for independence.

Prior to his arrest, Collins had been on his way from Canada (where he was training troops for WWI) to Houston to check on his oil deal when he was apprehended in the Grunewald Hotel (later, The Roosevelt) in New Orleans and incarcerated in the House of Detention there.

Thus began a five-year battle against extradition to India. Collins hired Poe and Bartlett of Washington, highly respected American attorneys in the field of litigation in the federal courts and J. Zack Spearing, one of New Orleans best lawyers. They filed objections to the extradition procedures in every form imaginable, carrying the fight from the local district court to the Court of Appeals and then to the U.S. Supreme Court. On the third trip to the highest court, he finally lost his last chance of beating extradition. It was May 4, 1923, more than five years since his arrest in October 1917.

During that period, he was in and out of the House of Detention, reportedly more out than in. He was granted bond several times, and it is believed that even when under detention he was allowed to come and go almost at will since he had gotten to know his jailors so well. They were enamored with his charm and wit and his intriguing stories of his war adventures.

Collins loved the social whirl of the Crescent City. His mystique and charm made him the darling of many of the society matrons and he became the centerpiece guest of many social events in the St. Charles Avenue homes. He also frequented the exclusive men's clubs such as The Boston Club where he enjoyed dinner, poker, brandy, and cigars with the prominent businessmen and bankers of the city. It was there he became acquainted with John W. McGrath, son of the founder of the department store chain begun in Brookhaven. He was occasionally a guest in the home of Mr. & Mrs. McGrath and was assisted by Mr. McGrath when he needed to renew his bond.

He also became friends of the literary set in the city, which included Sherwood Anderson, William Spratling, and William Faulkner. He was especially fond of Faulkner, a struggling young writer who had recently had his first novel published. Collins would occasionally pick him up in his Cadillac to play golf. Faulkner was

Mississippi Gumbo

both intrigued and puzzled by this character Collins. He had written his mother about this unusual individual, but expressing doubts as to the many tales he told about his war experiences in Africa and Gallipoli and about the royal family and other world figures. But a few weeks later in another letter he said, "No, Col. Collins is a fact. We played golf yesterday, and he had just this minute called me and invited me to a party at a Mississippi lady's this afternoon."

An avid gambler, Collins once won about $100,000 at the Fairgrounds Race Track and immediately bought a yacht, dubbed the *Josephine* docked at Lake Ponchatrain. He quickly invited his jailors and guards to enjoy a leisurely cruise on the lake.

Later he took the literary crowd including Faulkner on a wild three-day excursion on Ponchatrain, exploring all its nooks and crannies. The yacht became stuck and grounded in some shallow water at one point on the north side of the lake. While the ship and crew were waiting for help, Faulkner sought some fun and adventure, slipping away in the yacht's small dinghy, taking a young lass from the yacht with him who also craved adventure. They paddled to the North shore and attempted to walk through the dismal swamp to the little town of Mandeville where they had heard there were some interesting bars and saloons. However, they eventually gave up due to the swarms of mosquitoes and exhaustion and finally found a grizzly swamp dweller who, for a fee, gave them a motorboat ride back to the yacht. This wild Ponchatrain voyage inspired his second novel, a fictionalized account of the unforgettable adventure on the

Josephine. Appropriately, the book was entitled <u>Mosquitoes</u>. Collins is portrayed in the novel as an English officer, Major Ayers.

When the string had run out in his legal fight and he was to leave on an ocean liner to England, accompanied by a Scotland Yard detective, the now famous Colonel Collins was given a tremendous send off by his many friends in New Orleans. A jazz band played at the dock, and the crowd cheered and waved. He made a moving speech thanking them for their support and friendship, and promising to return as soon as the little inconvenience of his life or death trial was out of the way.

When in London he attempted to appeal to King George for help. Collins had known the king when he was Prince of Wales. Collins had been a young captain in the Scottish Highlanders Cameron Regiment, and after the unit's return from the Boer War in 1902, they were assigned to Balmoral Castle in Scotland to attend to the needs of King Edward VII on a royal family holiday for six weeks. Collins had taken the Prince on a grouse hunt where they shared a hunting stand. They enjoyed each other's company, and Collins asked the Prince to be the regiment's "Colonel in Chief," an honorary position formerly held by Queen Victoria. The prince was flattered and had gladly accepted.

Thus, Collins now had high hopes for help from his old hunting mate who had risen to be the sovereign of the British Empire. Unfortunately, the issue of the Collins case was a hot potato between Britain and India. The English were desperate to keep India in the empire, and the Indians, under Gandhi's encouragement, were flaunting the Collins case as one where the English were taking advantage of their poor colonists. This predicament was explained to Collins, and he was taken to India for the trial with little hope for success against what seemed to be a stacked deck.

Newspaper reports relate, however, that the juries in the two trials were composed of an equal number of Indian natives and Europeans. With his astute Washington lawyers assisted by local colonial attorneys, Collins surprisingly won acquittal on all charges and returned to New Orleans triumphantly. It is not known whether the equal balance in the jury composition was the result of diplomatic negotiations with the King's backing or not, but one would speculate that that may have been the case.

The African Wars

Charles Glen Collins was born April 19, 1880, the third son of Alexander Glen Collins and wife, Cornelia Thompson Collins, in Glasgow, Scotland. His family was quite wealthy as a result of the publishing company, Collins and Sons, founded by his grandfather, Sir William Collins, which had become the largest publishing house in the British empire—with offices in India, Australia, and other British colonies.

In the late 1890's, Britain was having problems in Africa maintaining its colonies there. The Dark Continent was rising in economic importance as the Suez Canal was being completed, and Britain faced competition for dominance from France, Belgium, the

Netherlands, and Germany. By 1897, England desperately needed to beef up its military forces to put down uprising in the Soudan, and to maintain its control of South Africa, Egypt, and other areas. They sought to maintain control of a wide path across the continent from South Africa northeastward to Cairo, controlling the Nile and the Red Sea.

Scotland was a good source of officers and men for the army. It had several historic regiments steeped in tradition. There were six kilted Highland regiments, two of these were "Royal Highland Regiments," the Camerons and the "Black Watch." To become a member of these prestigious regiments, one had to be from a distinguished family background before one's name was submitted for approval of the Sovereign.

Collins entered the Royal Military College at Sandhurst in 1897 and was commissioned a second lieutenant a year later and assigned to the "Queen's Own Highland Camerons." The regiment was already in the Soudan, Africa, and he was posted to the first battalion.

He went to London at once to see about his uniforms and equipment. The regimental tailors had him all ready to go in 48 hours, and he set sail on a troop ship for Cairo.

The British, with the Egyptians, were trying to suppress a rebellion of the Dervishes in the Soudan, which had started some twenty years earlier and had culminated in the murder of General Charles Gordon at Khartoum in 1885, which had outraged the English people and fueled their resolve to squelch the Soudanese.

General Sir Herbert Kitchener commanded the British forces against the Khalifa, the native chief, whose Dervishes fought like fanatics and believed if they killed an unbeliever they would go to heaven.

Kitchener received intelligence of the location of a large encampment of the enemy, some 70,000 strong, on the banks of the Atbara River twenty miles from the Nile. He decided on a swift march and a surprise attack. The Dervishes were caught by surprise, and 7,000 casualties were inflicted and 15,000 prisoners were captured.

Collins' Camerons led the attack and lost less than 100 men. The British had been told that the enemy camp was protected by a high zareba (stockade) of thorny acacia, and the troops had been issued scaling ladders. However, it turned out that the zareba was only two or three feet tall and could easily be jumped.

After the attack began, many of the natives feigned death inside their camp and waited until they had a chance to jump up and kill an infidel. One of the victims of this ruse was Captain Charles Findlay of the Camerons. He had led his company, hurdled the zareba, turned, and waved to his men to follow when a Dervish leaped up and ran him through with a spear before his outraged men could dispatch him.

Queen Victoria had been especially fond of this officer, became the godmother of his posthumous child, and appointed the young widow, who had been married but six months, to be one of her ladies-in-waiting. Three years later when the young widow considered remarrying, the Queen sent for her and gave her quite a scolding, for the powerful Queen had remained celibate for thirty years after her prince consort's death, and she didn't approve of widows taking a second husband.

The regiment had a great deal of idle time between occasional engagements with the enemy. The life of a young officer in the regiment appears in retrospect to be more like a vacation than combat. Collins was athletic. He had been a star athlete in school and had become an avid polo player. He and other officers were able to purchase fine Arabian horses from Bedouin traders. The officers would buy young colts at about $35 each and train them for polo. Collins bought four and employed two stable hands to look after them. Polo matches were held weekly.

Besides polo, Collins enjoyed traveling to the sights and cities of Egypt and also a bit of duck hunting on the Nile. Collins was invited to several big shooting parties on the several thousand acres of swamplands in the Nile delta owned by Prince Kam-el-Din. Some forty or so hunters would leave on a special train at two a.m., and after an hour's run, the train would stop every few minutes to let out two men, who with their shikaris, each carrying two guns and about five hundred rounds of ammunition, would proceed to their "butts," or blinds in the bull rushes. It was planned that every man would be in a blind before dawn. As soon as all were in place, the orders were to begin firing. Every piece of water was literally covered with ducks. As soon as the shooting began, the birds in the tens of thousands would fly frantically in every direction. One fired both barrels until they grew too hot to handle, and the guns were constantly being handed back to the shikari to reload. In about 30 minutes, the birds flew too high, and one had time to gather the kills and to put out decoys. Then the hunting became more sporting as the decoys and calls were used to lure the ducks into range.

When the sun and temperature rose, the hunters retired to a camp for lunch and bull sessions. Then at four o'clock, the ducks began to return, and the hunt resumed until dusk. At six o'clock, the locomotive returned and signaled the hunters to gather. The average bag for a hunt was twelve hundred to two thousand brace of duck.

The kilts worn by the Scottish regiments are a source of pride to them. Collins stated in his diary:

> There are three sets of kilts. Those for winter, for summer, and for dancing. A kilt or skirt is really a survival of the costume worn, instead of trousers, by the Highlanders in the native hills. The heather of the Scottish moor and glens is high and the crags of the Scottish Mountains so precipitous that the ancient clansmen found it more comfortable to wear these kilts than the trousers of other countries. Nowadays, the Highland Regiments are very proud of their kilts and would probably stage mutiny rather than discard them. In the Soudan, Dervish prisoners told us that they all implicitly believed that the reason why our Regiment had attacked them with such gallantry and ferocity was because we had had our trousers taken away from us in some previous war, owing to cowardice, and were made to dress like women, and that the trousers would only be restored when the proof of new courage had been shown. This legend still persists in Equatorial Africa.

> The kilt is made of heavy or light woolen tartan material some four yards long and one yard wide. It is fastened by means of two buckles on the hips. It must be long enough to come to the middle of the kneecap. This length is determined by kneeling: when the bottom must just graze the floor. Apart from its value as "showy" piece of uniform, it possesses real value in that it gives you a pleasant sense of freedom when marching or running. In the summer, it is airy and cool, and, in the winter, the wide belt of woolen material keeps the stomach warm. It was found out in the Crimean War, the Boer War and the late World War that kilted troops very rarely contract dysentery or cholera.
>
> The kilt in its manufacture is so made or "weighted" that it will only swing when walking or dancing to a certain height and thus avoid indecent exposure. The dancing kilt is really a work of art, as it is made in such a way as to enable one to dance in comfort and still not shock spectators. I have often been asked by the curious what is worn underneath the kilt. No Highland Officer or man ever wears any drawers, but the Regimental Pipers, who give exhibition dances on raised stages, occasionally do wear on those occasions, very short tartan under-drawers.

Once Collins was the subject of a subaltern's court martial (actually sort of a kangaroo court) for improperly wearing his kilt at a dance the previous night while seated on a sofa. He had shown some three inches or so more of his legs than was right and proper.

Collins related that on Sir Ian Hamilton's staff were two famous cousins, the Duke of Marlborough and Winston S. Churchill, who were billeted next to Collins' regiment. His companions were entertained by observing that the Duke invariably did all the dirty work—pitching and striking their tent, cooking and cleaning the pots and pans while his cousin smoked his pipe and freely criticized him. Collins learned that rarely do the men with brains do any work in this world.

Collins often traveled around the area during inactive times. Once he was visiting in Alexandria and attending an open-air café where a traveling Italian opera troupe was performing. Present was Captain Arthur Egerton of the Camerons who was an opera enthusiast and friend of the Impresario of the Cairo Opera House. He was impressed with a 22-year-old tenor in the troupe and asked the manager to invite him to their table for a glass of wine. The young singer complied, and Egerton asked him if he would like for him to speak to his Cairo friend on his behalf. The young tenor was Enrico Caruso who eagerly accepted the help and became the star of the Cairo Opera and from thence to worldwide fame.

A puzzling entry in the records of the West Indies Cricket organization shows that Collins participated in the 1901-02 season, playing for Jamaica. It lists his record of batting, fielding and bowling. There is no reference in his papers explaining how he managed to cross the Atlantic and play cricket during or between the wars in Africa.

Robert E. Jones

The Boer War

Shortly after the Soudanese campaign was successfully concluded, the British had to deal with the Boer conflict in South Africa. General Kitchener was in command of the British forces and moved his headquarters to the South. Collins was made adjutant under Kitchener.

One of the Boer commanders was a particular thorn in the side of Kitchener's campaign. He was General Beyers. Kitchener was anxious to get rid of this particular opponent and offered a reward of a hundred cattle to be given to the man or men who could capture the general.

At the time, there were a large number of Texans fighting for Kitchener. They had boarded ships headed for South Africa as workers and then deserted when it arrived in port in order to get in the fight. Things had more or less quieted down in Texas since the Civil War, and they wanted action.

After learning of the reward for Beyers, a number of the Americans went AWOL from their units; and several days later three Texans came riding up and proudly reporting to Collins, the adjutant, that they had got Beyers. They told how they had rushed a farmhouse at night after a fight in which two of their men were killed, and they had shot and slain three Boers. They said they were too far away to haul the entire body of General Beyers back to camp and solved the problem by removing his head and putting it in a horse's nosebag. They then triumphantly produced the grisly evidence. Unfortunately, for all, it was not General Beyers, although there was a slight resemblance, but close didn't count.

Collins ordered them to bury the head right away and to keep their mouths shut. Later when Collins told Kitchener about it, he laughed and commented he was glad the neutral press never got wind of the story.

While serving in an infantry company early in the conflict with the Boers, the unit was temporarily housed in barracks. The men were routinely aroused to "stand at arms" a half hour before daybreak. The officer of the day and the color sergeant would pass down the aisle between the bunks and each soldier would extend a leg straight out from under his blanket to show he was awake, then when the officer and sergeant had reached the end of the aisle, the sergeant would command all to arise at attention.

One morning when Collins, as officer of the day, had just finished the wake up inspection, there was a loud frantic call for help from the other end of the aisle. One soldier was holding his leg out from his bed and there, neatly coiled around his ankle was a big fat snake, with its head resting on the soldier's shinbone and its beady eyes silently staring at the lad. Collins immediately recognized the serpent as the dreaded "puff adder" whose bite is fatal within minutes. The situation was delicate as to how to get the intruder away from the victim without provoking a strike.

A long mop handle was secured, and slowly and gently, it was used to uncoil the snake from the trembling leg, while a cocked rifle was held aimed at the snake's head for a last resort. A large bucket of water was placed alongside the bunk, and finally the snake was lifted and dropped into the pail, much to the relief of all. Collins ordered the men to take the bucket outside and dispose of the unwelcome visitor.

The young soldiers impulsively started to have sport with the bucketed snake, taking turns trying to jab him with bayonets. This was great sport until the snake became infuriated and managed to lunge and struck one of the men on the forearm. Aghast, the men rushed him to the regimental doctor's wagon, but he died within ten minutes. Nothing could be done. Collins was severely reprimanded for not making sure the snake was properly disposed of.

Another time after his unit had made camp after an exhaustive twenty-mile march, guards were routinely posted for the night around the camp. One twenty-year-old recruit was stationed as sentry at one corner of the camp perimeter. He was weary from the long hot march and had been suffering from a toothache for several days but had not asked to be excused from guard duty. When the visiting major from the camp inspected the guards at four a.m., he found the lad in a deep slumber. Collins could not persuade the major to let the matter be handled within the company. The staff office insisted on making an example from this "flagrant sleeping on sentry duty in the face of the enemy."

A general court-martial was held a few days later. Collins testified for the boy and pleaded extenuating circumstances, but the stern wartime rules were followed, and the lad was convicted and sentenced to be shot. However, upon review at Kitchener's headquarters, the sentence was commuted to penal servitude for life. The sentence was pronounced before the entire assembled regiment drawn up on parade. The unfortunate lad was sent to work on a breakwater with other military prisoners. The whole affair broke his spirit. Two years later at the end of the war, the Queen pardoned all military prisoners in the African campaign. When the army was ready to return home, Collins quickly went to the prison to give the boy the good news, but he had become so bitter that he angrily told Collins he could "go to hell along with the whole damn British army."

Probably the most interesting character Collins encountered in this campaign was Colonel Johon, the fiery commander of the Kitchener Fighting Scouts. He was the son of a wealthy Dutch sugar planter who had come to Natal in 1851. His name had been Brander, but after he had run away from home at 15 years of age and joined a Zulu chief called Cotewayo, he changed his name to a Zulu name and lived with the tribe for 18 years. The chief more or less adopted the white boy, made him his companion, and showered him with gifts of cattle.

When the Zulus began to harass and murder white settlers in the area, Johon repeatedly warned them against antagonizing the great white Queen. When the trouble continued, Johon left Zululand, sold his herd of 3,000 cattle for 20,000 pounds, and moved several hundred miles away to Masholand in the late 1880's. There he met Cecil Rhodes, who had amassed an immense fortune from diamonds. Rhodes and Johon became close friends and business associates, and Johon's own fortune grew to a sizeable sum.

Johon was of great assistance to the famous man. Rhodes had become fluent in many of the native languages, but Johon was probably the greatest linguist in South Africa. In 1894, the natives of Masholand gave trouble to the white farmers and ranchers and continued to do violence to them. Strong mounted columns of well-equipped men were recruited to quell the uprising, but Rhodes hated the prospect of bitter and severe fighting. He determined to attempt to bring about a sound peace between the factions by negotiations with the native tribes. He took Johon and another negotiator, and rode under a white flag long distances deep into the Matbelias territory. A grand "Indaba" was held, squatting on the ground with Johon interpreting. After many days of hard negotiation, a peace was arranged. Nothing was signed, since the tribes had no written language, and the agreement, wholly verbal, was sealed by handshakes. Thereafter, none of the terms of peace were ever violated by either side.

When the Boer War broke out, Rhodes suggested to Kitchener that Johon could be of service to him. Johon had grown up hunting, riding, and fighting with the Zulus and was very skilled in those pursuits. After Kitchener asked for Johon's help, in one week he recruited an entire regiment of mounted native warriors to fight for the British. He was granted permission to use Kitchener's name for his regiment—hence Kitchener's Fighting Scouts.

Collins, as staff officer under Kitchener, was present at numerous conferences between Kitchener and Johon. He was amazed at the temerity of Johon who would scold Kitchener occasionally for blunders and put forth bold plans of his own ideas, which were invariably adopted by Kitchener.

Johon was known for his horsemanship and marksmanship. Frequently on treks across the open lands, he would spot a gazelle or other wild animal at a distance and gallop at full speed after the fleeing prey and quickly pull his rifle and bring down the running target at 100 to 200 yards with a single shot.

In mid June 1900, a major battle of the war was fought about 20 miles east of Pretoria centered around a long hill known as Diamond Hill since the precious stones had been discovered there some time before. A few years later, the world was stunned by the discovery of a gigantic quality diamond the size of a man's fist. A rough uneducated Irishman named Cullinan found it. It was eventually cut up and the largest piece became the central stone of the Royal British crown. That stone was valued in 1900 at over 200,000 pounds. No insurance company would insure it's shipment to England, so it was packed in a small box and mailed uninsured to England while a dummy stone was sent off with much fanfare and fuss and guarded in the most careful manner. The real diamond arrived safely.

The strategy that helped end the Boer War adopted by Kitchener was a sort of scorched earth policy. The British would raid the farms and ranches of the Boers while the men were off fighting and take the women and children for internment in concentration camps and burn and destroy the farm or ranch. This practice was widely condemned, however, some of the Boer farmers were actually relieved by it since they had been fearful that the marauding natives would attack their farms and slaughter their families. They felt their dependents would be safer in the hands of the British concentration camps. However, when peace finally prevailed, the British government appropriated three million pounds to rebuild the destroyed properties of the Boers.

Collins Serves the King at Balmoral Castle

After the Boer War was concluded, Charles Glen Collins sailed to England on the *Killdonian Castle*, docking at Southampton on July 25, 1902. His father, mother, older brother and his sister joyously greeted him.

His family excitedly told him all of the news, particularly that Lord Kitchener had mentioned him in his final war dispatch and that he had been promoted to Brevet-Major. The big news was that he was just in time for the coronation of King Edward that day.

Collins' father had gotten a pass for his son to the ceremony in the Westminster Abbey and had brought his uniform case containing his full dress uniform.

Collins and his father attended the spectacular pageantry of the coronation. Especially impressive were the peers of the throne in their scarlet and ermine capes.

The coronation had been delayed for several weeks due to an illness of the new king. Gypsies had prophesied that he would never be crowned, and bookies were taking bets on whether or not he would make it. However, he managed to take the throne and keep it for some eighteen years.

A few days later, Collins went with his father to Norway on their yacht the *Gladys*. Collins had many fond memories as a youth sailing on the *Gladys* around the English coast, in the Mediterranean Sea, and in Norwegian waters.

When they returned from their Norwegian visit, Collins received a telegram from Edinburgh ordering him to report at once to join the King's guard at Balmoral Castle. Every year when the royal family takes its late summer holiday, they have one of the Highland Regiments to serve as their guard of honor. This was quite a pleasant duty, waiting on the King, grouse hunting, dining with the royalty, and meeting the many distinguished guests from the royal courts of Europe and elsewhere.

One of the first visitors was Lord Kitchener, the national hero of the African campaigns, with whom Collins was well acquainted.

When Collins was in London getting his uniforms ready to go to Balmoral Castle, he took on a new gadget for fun—a new motorcar. He paid six hundred pounds for a "Panhard Levassor" two cylinder, with a coach made by Hooper. He had never seen a motorcar until the day he was leaving Cape Town to return home.

He hired a French chauffer to drive it to Aberdeen. It nearly resulted in a disaster later when he was driving it along a narrow trail near the castle and came suddenly upon a carriage containing the Princess of Wales and her five children. The horses panicked at the strange noisy contraption, and a major accident on the mountainside was narrowly averted. Collins jumped out of his car, managed to grab the bridle of one of the horses, and calmed them down, thereby preventing them from backing the carriage over the steep drop off at the edge of the trail. Later it was politely suggested to Collins that the motorcar would best be left in Aberdeen for the rest of his stay.

The Queen Alexandria was absent at first, visiting her father at Copenhagen, the King of Denmark. She met her sister there also, the Czarina of Russia.

Collins had great sport grouse hunting. Some seventy beaters would run the grouse to the line of "butts" (hunting stands). Once Collins shared a butt with the Prince of Wales (later King George V) and offered him the honorary position of "Colonel in Chief" of his Highland Camerons Regiment. The prince accepted with pleasure. They had a fine hunt together and became friends. Later in Collins' subsequent troubles, he asked for help from his friend who was then King—but that comes later.

The dinners at the castle were not as formal as at the palace. Collins wrote the following:

> The guests would all assemble in the drawing room a few minutes before nine o'clock. All the men would wear formal evening dress, tail coats and white ties except instead of trousers they would wear knee breeches like silk stockings and black patent leather pumps with silver buckles. All Scotsmen at the party would wear Kilts. As soon as the King arrives in the drawing room, one of the requisites was introduced to him and any new arrivals at the castle as well as any guests from surrounding country houses. Immediately

a procession lead by the King moved into the dining room where the guests who have been cautioned beforehand as to their places, would seat themselves without any delay. King Edward was a great epicure. He loved his food and his cook, to whom he paid over two thousand pounds a year. At the same time, he broke the old established fashion of remaining at the dining table for two hours and possibly longer. Five courses only would be served: soup, fish, entrée, roast and sweets. A still white wine was served with the fish and the wine butlers offered the guests choice of champagne, claret, or malmsey, just before the roast was served. There was a footman to every two guests. These men, admirably trained, insured a rapid service. One of the wine butlers, Donald Cameron, used to be the wine butler of the Camerons. He had greeted me affectionately when I arrived, and he made a point at a dinner party to stand behind me and was always whispering in my ear his advice as to which wine I should select.

After one dinner when the King and guests had retired to the drawing room for liqueur, conversation and bridge, the Duke of Allanby, a Spaniard and close friend of the King of Spain, was invited by King Edward to join in a game of bridge.

The Spaniard appeared unsure but felt he must comply, although he barely knew the basics of the game. The King loved to gamble and usually played for a pound per point. After a few hands, the King's voice was heard in a loud, harsh tone, "You have revoked!" The Duke, partner of the King, was painfully embarrassed. A few hands later the King again showed his displeasure saying, "We think you had better try your luck at another table." The other players were Arthur Sassoon, a man of great wealth, and Arthur Balfour, the foreign secretary.

King Edward was fond of the French and had engineered the informal understanding between the two nations known as the "Entente Cordiale" which basically was a "live and let live" attitude between them and was the basis for settling the Fashoda confrontation on the upper Nile.

However, he despised his cousin, Kaiser Wilhelm of Germany, who claimed that he was the rightful king of England since his mother had been the oldest child of Queen Victoria. This infuriated Edward.

King Edward made some changes at the castle. The first was pertaining to the statue of John Brown, which had been erected by his mother. John Brown of Abyssinia had been the "gillie" or personal servant of the Queen after the death of her Prince Consort Albert. She had become very close and dependent upon him, which gave rise to vicious rumors. Edward had the granite monument taken down and sent to Brown's family seventy miles away.

At the end of Collins' tour at Balmoral, the physician in attendance, Sir James Reed, who was a family friend, called Collins aside and told him he needed a complete rest for several months. The doctor gave him a certificate to give to his colonel, which resulted in a six months sick leave. He had been diagnosed as suffering from Bright's disease.

It was the custom of the Collins family that each child upon reaching his majority would be given an around the world trip. Thus, arrangements were made for a sea voyage for Collins and his sister, Cornelia, and a few days later, they sailed on the *Caris-brook* for Cape Town to start their west to east circle of the globe.

Collins Meets World's Strongest Man and World's Most Beautiful Girl

After the memorable month's tour of duty at Balmoral Castle in the Scottish highlands, serving King Edward VII, Collins received a six months medical leave due to a diagnosis of Bright's disease. His family followed their custom of giving a round the world trip to each child upon reaching their majority, and Collins and his older sister, Cornelia, set sail on the *Caris-Brooke* for Cape Town.

After a fortnight's visit in South Africa, the two continued their voyage stopping in Hobart, Tasmania, thence to Sydney and spent two weeks in Australia including a stay at a huge sheep ranch where Collins enjoyed riding fast horses hunting kangaroo.

Next came a stay over in New Zealand and a bit of polo playing.

After embarking on the ship bound for San Francisco via Honolulu, they became acquainted with another passenger, Eugen Sandow, who styled himself the "strongest man in the world." He was a showman who had performed his act in Sydney and was scheduled for another in San Francisco.

When the ship stopped at one of the Pago Pago islands, Rayago, to deliver mail, the passengers were allowed to disembark and mingle with the natives in their village. When Sandow was challenged to display his strength to the natives, he selected the largest hut in the village, grabbed the center bamboo pole, and hoisted the entire hut above his head. It happened to be the hut of the chief who was away visiting the docked ship at the time. The natives were terrified at this and fled into the jungle for fear of what the chief might do.

After an idyllic two weeks stay in Honolulu, they headed for Frisco and finally steamed through the Golden Gate Bridge in February. Collins met Sandow in the lobby of the Bally Hotel the next day and was invited to attend a dress rehearsal of a stunt he was to perform that night. The stunt involved wrestling a lion, and the local SPCA demanded to witness the rehearsal before allowing a permit.

The theater had a large cage where reposed a huge, irritable African lion. Wisely, the beast had been fitted with padded gloves and wore a strong leather muzzle. When Sandow stepped into the cage, the lion immediately expressed his displeasure and sprang at him, but Sandow nimbly stepped aside. The lion turned and furiously charged the strong man, who again easily avoided the charge and quickly grabbed the cat around the body as he passed. Sandow fixed his feet firmly, and with a mighty heave, threw the lion over his shoulders violently to the floor. With the lion momentarily dazed, Sandow stepped out of the cage triumphantly.

The SPCA was satisfied and allowed the show to proceed that night. However, the night's performance was not one of the highlights of Sandow's career. When the time came in the show for the big finish—the battle between man and lion—Sandow stepped heroically into the lion's cage, but instead of a fierce charge, the lion apparently had had enough of that game and refused to participate. Sandow had to chase the subdued lion around the cage for several minutes before he could catch and throw him to the floor where the poor creature lay on his back with his paws in the air completely docile. The audience was furious, booing and throwing things and nearly wrecked the theater.

Sandow, however, went on to worldwide fame, and today is remembered at the international annual strongman competition where the winner is presented a statuette of Eugen Sandow. (See more on the net at www.sandowmuseum.com.)

Collins and Cornelia enjoyed the Frisco area, particularly the Del Monte resort, and its golf course which had been open only five years, now known as Pebble Beach.

A visit to the Grand Canyon was also a highlight. Collins commented in his memoirs that there are only two places he would go out of his way to visit: the Taj Mahal at Agra in India at sunset and the Grand Canyon at daybreak.

The travelers crossed the country and wound up in the Waldorf Astoria in New York. Their wealthy American cousins entertained Cornelia for the next month or so, and Collins made the rounds of house parties and polo games.

He had met a charming heiress, "Alice," who had fallen for him, and he was pleased with her, but not head over heels in love.

Robert E. Jones

She had planned a dinner party on a Monday to introduce Collins to her friends. However, Collins had gone to Lakewood, New Jersey, for a weekend at George Gould's estate for a polo party. The Gould country estate was designed for lovers of sport. Two large polo fields and great numbers of Polo ponies were available for their guests. There was a large covered riding school with miniature jumps, a racket court, tennis court, two squash racket courts, several lawn tennis courts, a large covered swimming pool and an elaborate Turkish bath. Among the girls present was Miss Nathalie Schenck, of whom Collins said he had never seen any one so beautiful as she. She was the leading belle of New York City and Newport. On Saturday, he had a slight accident when his horse fell and rolled over his leg, but did little harm. The New York Herald reported this accident, but he telephoned Alice and assured her he would make the dinner.

However, one small incident unavoidably prevented him from attending Alice's dinner—he met Nathalie Schenck and fell instantly in love with her. He danced with her several times Sunday night and was easily persuaded to stay over for Monday's polo match. He telegraphed Alice that he was suffering from his polo accident and could not possibly be back until Tuesday.

He might have gotten away with the lie, but for the article on the society page of the Herald reporting that he had scored the winning goal in the Monday polo match and was in attendance with Miss Schenck at the dance that night. This ended his affair with Alice.

Mississippi Gumbo

On Tuesday, his infatuation with Nathalie deepened. They were riding to New York from the Gould's on the coach of James Hazenhyde (principal owner of Equitable Life) when they decided to ride on the top of the coach. A rainstorm came up, and they huddled closely under a tarpaulin to stay dry, but enjoyed the cuddling so much they continued under the wrap long after the rain had stopped. He was smitten.

He had to leave America shortly thereafter and sailed on the *Celtic* for home. On the voyage, he met J.P. Morgan and was asked to join his table for bridge, but his thoughts were with the memory of the coach ride in the rain with the beautiful Nathalie.

However, he managed to cope quite well. He said in his memoirs he spent a lot of time in Paris:

> "During the summer of 1903, on several occasions I made flying visits to Paris. My program in Paris was pretty much the same on all occasions. I would get up about nine in the morning, don riding clothes and taxi out to the entrance of the Bois where a horse would be waiting for me. I would then ride leisurely, trotting and cantering, around the Bois, stop at Pre Catalan for a cocktail around eleven o'clock and wind up shortly after noon at Armenorville for lunch. I have always found the cooking at Armenorville, Paillard's and the Chateau de Madrid, the best in Paris and consequently the best in the world. After luncheon, I would return to the hotel and take a car to the nearest racecourse. After drinking a number of cocktails before dinner, I would dine either at the Larue, Paillard's, the Marguery or the Café de Anglais then take in a theater, preferably the Gymnase or the Lo'Odeon or the Opera Comic."

A charming French girl came into his acquaintance, and he dallied with her for three months in a torrid affair. He had to break up with her when his commanding officer criticized the business. Collins learned that she wound up as the mistress of Bruno Rothschild-Goldsmith, one of the secretaries of the German Embassy in London and one of Europe's wealthiest men. She later told Collins that when Rothschild got married he settled on her two thousand pounds a year and title to a charming maisonette in Paris.

When Collins read in the Paris edition of the New York Herald that the yacht *Varuna* with its owner Mr. Eugene Higgins had just arrived in Cannes with a large party aboard including Mrs. Pottswood Schenck and her daughter Nathalie, he ordered his valet to book him on that night's train to Cannes.

After making contact with her at her hotel, she greeted him with a smile and "I surely am glad to see you again, Captain Collins," which moment he says is his most cherished memory.

He joined the party on the yacht *Varuna* and sailed around Sicily and Sardinia before returning to Cannes. By the end of the cruise, they were determined to marry. Nathalie explained that although she was the granddaughter of Matthew Morgan II, formerly one of the leading investment bankers of New York, she had no income at all, and the family had been poor since the banking house's failure fifteen years earlier. Of course, this made little difference to Collins since his family owned the largest publishing house in the

British Empire. They agreed to be engaged and that Collins would follow her back to America.

After Collins and Nathalie Schenck had found fervent love in the Mediterranean, they announced their engagement to the delight of Nathalie's mother, Mrs. Spottswood Schenck. They decided to leave for America right away.

Collins' doctor had advised him that his affliction of Bright's disease was worsening, and he should take another long rest on six months leave from his regiment.

After arriving in New York, the news of the engagement was reported in the Herald and a rush from Nathalie's friends and family overwhelmed them. Nathalie's closest friend, Mrs. Reginald Vanderbilt, entertained them lavishly.

After three days in New York, they left for Del Monte in California for a quiet rest. Collins' was physically exhausted, and Nathalie suggested that she could nurse him back to health better if they were married right away. So a quick, small wedding was planned. A small party of relatives and friends came from the East to attend, among them Nathalie's uncles, Matthew and George Morgan, and her uncle by marriage, Mr. August Belmont, who had been married to Mrs. Schenck's sister who had recently died in Paris.

The only bridal attendant was Mrs. Reginald (Catherine) Vanderbilt. A year earlier, Nathalie had been a bridesmaid at Catherine's wedding.

Robert E. Jones

The wedding took place at the Del Monte resort. It was reported in the New York Times as follows:

"MISS NATHALIE SCHENCK WEDS.

Quietly Married in California to Capt.
Glen Collins of the British Army.

Special to The New York Times
PACIFIC GROVE, Cal., April 7—Miss Nathalie P. Schenck of New York was married about 9 o'clock this morning in the Episcopal Chapel, attached to the Del Monte Hotel, to Capt. Glen Collins, who served with the British Army in the Boer war.

Two weeks ago, the bride-elect and her mother, Mrs. Schenck, arrived at the hotel. This morning the only thing known of the wedding was that accommodations had been engaged on tonight's train for Santa Barbara, and that rooms had been booked at the Palmer House there for "Capt. Collins and wife."

It was supposed that the wedding would take place about noon today. Last night the Rev. John A. Emory arrived from San Francisco, and was met by Capt. Collins and escorted to a room occupied by the party. While Del Monte was at breakfast this morning, there was a very quiet wedding in the chapel, with "Nobody there," to use Mrs. Schenck's words, but the Newport beauty and her mother, the groom, and the necessary witnesses.

After the ceremony, the bride and her mother awaited a southbound train at Del Monte Station. Capt. Collins joining them just after the cars drew up. The bride wore a white lace-trimmed picture hat and a white dress almost concealed by a long black coat. Mrs. Schenck, after waving the young couple farewell, returned to the hotel."

Mississippi Gumbo

A week later, the New York Times carried a curious story about the formalities of the wedding announcement. The parents of the bride were separated and not on good terms to say the least. The story noted that two different versions of the wedding had been submitted: one referring to Nathalie as the daughter of Mrs. Spottswood Schenck, and the other as the daughter of Spottswood Schenck Esq. They also disagreed on the spelling of her name—Nathalie versus Nathalia. Anyway, the marriage license records that Nathalie Pendleton Cutting Schenck of New York was duly married to Charles Glen Collins of Scotland on April 7, 1904.

The license also lists as one of the witnesses Charles Innis Kerr of London. This latter individual had a special interest in Collins. About a month before the couple left Europe Kerr had gone to Collins' apartment one morning for a purpose. Collins knew Mr. Kerr as the grandson of the Duchess of Roxdurah who was probably Queen Victoria's closest personal friend. Kerr had been an accepted person in the royal court. Twenty years older than Collins, Kerr was an impressive and persuasive experienced businessman, while young Collins had had little training or experience in financial matters.

After enjoying a drink and some small talk, Kerr told Collins about a huge real estate deal he had arranged and that he was going to make an enormous sum from it. However, he was having a little problem raising the necessary funds to close it, but all he needed was for someone like Collins to sign the back of a few notes for him. Collins' family trust fund was set to release to him his shares in the publishing house in a few weeks. Kerr cheerfully told Collins that the matter was of a trivial nature and that he would give Collins three thousand pounds from the loan, so Collins could have plenty of funds for his honeymoon. The naïve groom was happy to oblige such an important friend as Mr. Kerr and endorsed 15 notes of two thousand pounds each. True to his word, Kerr brought Collins three thousand pounds in cash the next day.

The happy couple spent a short honeymoon in a cottage at Santa Barbara, and Collins' health improved. They decided to sail for England by way of the Pacific and the Suez Canal and make a leisurely trip of it, with a week in Honolulu and a short stay in Japan. They sailed on the *Mongolia* from Frisco in May. In Hawaii, they were having a delightful time, and Collins got to play a little polo again. However, things began to take a bad turn when Nathalie was injured in a carriage accident after the horses had panicked and ran wild. She was not seriously injured but had to rest up for a while.

Then a bombshell in the form of a cablegram arrived from Collins' father in London, asking how many notes had he signed for Innis Kerr. Notes were arriving in alarming numbers, and Collins' immediate return home was advisable.

The couple sailed back to San Francisco and rode the train to New York where another message from his father told him not to come right away, as their lawyers were negotiating the matter with the moneylenders. The young couple decided to spend a month with the Vanderbilts at Sandy Point and then a month with August Belmont at his country home at Westbury, Long Island.

However, another cable arrived in July from the worried father telling Collins to come home right away, so they sailed and arrived in Southampton a week later. A family conference was held in Scotland with their lawyers. The bottom line was that Collins was to come into the family business and head one of the colonial offices. He would be able to make enough income to live comfortably and to pay off the moneylenders over a few years.

His father, Uncle William, and Aunt Elizabeth were charmed with Nathalie and pleased with the marriage even though the couple had not sought approval ahead of time. However, their opinion of the mother-in-law was a different story. They felt she was devious and conniving and mercenary, as well as unpleasant. Therefore, they attached one condition to their rescue offer—they were not to take the mother-in-law with them everywhere. They should live separately or else her presence and image would hurt the company and the marriage.

Collins and Nathalie rushed to Paris to confer with Mrs. Schenck and apparently, Collins didn't push hard enough to accept the deal, and it was turned down. So, he was left to cope with a huge financial problem on his own.

In the meanwhile, Mr. Innis Kerr, whose huge land deal never materialized, got himself out of the picture by putting a bullet through his forehead.

Collins decided to go back to Egypt where a boom was underway due to the recent completion of the Suez Canal. He made a deal with a Cairo banker friend to sniff out land deals to be bought in

Collins' name with the banker's money. This arrangement was working fairly well, and Nathalie, now pregnant, was enjoying life as a young housewife.

Things were going swimmingly with the eager Scot. He had made some good speculative buys on land and was profiting from trading in shares and securities. Money was coming in freely. Nathalie was expecting their offspring in the spring, and Collins had rented an apartment for her in Paris for three months to be near excellent medical facilities.

A few days before Christmas 1904, Collins was away on business and had to stay with some prospective land buyers over the holiday. After their negotiations ended, his Turkish friend, Tueny Bey, suggested they take in the races at Ghezirah. Collins couldn't resist. Some of his friends' horses were running that day, and with tips from them, he and Tueny won about 400 pounds each. Then came cocktails at the Savoy Hotel and dinner at the Khedevial Club, a very exclusive club of the wealthiest of Egyptians. Tueny was a member and got Collins a 30-day visitor's card. After several after dinner drinks, they wound up in the card room at about ten o'clock.

The Baccarat table lured the two young men. The dealer of the cards in Baccarat is whatever player has bid the most for the privilege and the other players bet against him as the Bank. The house collects a percentage of all bets. Collins and Tueny got lucky and had won quite a bit by 1:00 a.m., and when the bank was up for bids, they elected to try to get it jointly and did so.

Mississippi Gumbo

Their good luck continued after becoming the bank and they won some 12,000 pounds on the first four deals. Tueny begged Collins to cash in, but he insisted on continuing. They won the next deal, running their profit to 29,000 Louis or about 23,000 pounds (or $115,000). Tueny cashed in and pleaded with Collins to do so too. Each of them had started with only about 400 pounds and most of that were the racetrack winnings.

The other players became discouraged, and all decided to withdraw and not risk any more bets against the lucky Scot. However, Prince Mahomet Ibrahim, uncle of the Khedine, and Monsieur Edward Suarez, richest cotton broker in Egypt, who had been observing the action, took up the slack and offered to cover the entire amount of the bank, which was then 32,000 Louis.

The cards were dealt; Collins beat the challengers' hands, winning for the seventh consecutive deal. He now had over $250,000 in front of him. Tueny was frantic, whispering, "Cash in! Are you mad?" but Collins politely asked to the players "Vous voulez plus, Messieurs?" (Do you want any more gentlemen?) There was a quick consultation between the two remaining bettors, and finally after a nod from the Prince, Suarez huskily called out "Banquo!" meaning they would cover the entire amount of the bank, but the prince would play the hand. The other games in the huge room had ceased as all players gathered around the Baccarat table to view the startling contest between the brash Scot and the Egyptian prince. A tense hush befell the vast room. The heavy breathing of the contestants and the soft flutter of the shuffling cards were the only sounds.

Collins dealt himself a queen and a seven, a very good hand. The best hand is a total of eight or nine. Face cards and tens count zero. He announced he would take no more cards. The prince called for another card on each of his two hands, and Collins breathed more easily. He dealt the prince an eight on one hand and a trey on the other. Collins showed his hand and waited for the Prince to display his. On the first hand, the prince dramatically turned up two tens which gave him an eight count. On the other, he slowly revealed a queen and a five to go with the trey for another eight count, both hands beating Collins' seven count hand. The Scot had lost it all, his original stake, the racetrack winnings and the enormous pile from Baccarat. He forced a smile, shook hands around the table, and left for home.

When Collins reached home in the wee hours, Nathalie asked what he had been doing. He mumbled something about winning a little at the club, but didn't mention having lost a quarter million. When Nathalie later found out what had happened, she was dismayed since this was not the first such incident. She left and went to the apartment in Paris. Collins saw Nathalie only one more time when he and sister Cornelia stopped by on their way to London, but Nathalie was firm about the separation.

She returned to the states and divorced him, and he never saw his son, George Fessenden Collins. She remarried in 1909 to a New York stockbroker, William Laimbeer. Two daughters were born to them, but Mr. Laimbeer was killed in a car/train collision on Long

Island in 1913. Nathalie was injured badly and was a semi-invalid for several years thereafter.

She was determined however to do well and provide for her three small children even though she was well endowed by her deceased husband. Nathalie was very active in civic and charitable affairs performing responsible jobs during World War I. Afterwards, she embarked on a career in banking, reached the pinnacle of success with National City Bank, and helped found the Association of Bank Women, serving as its president three years.

Her son changed his name to George Morgan Laimbeer after the death of his stepfather. He became successful in the business world, serving for six years as Vice President and general manager of the Post division of General Foods and died in 1962. He had a grandson, Bill Laimbeer, who possibly inherited some physical traits from his tall and athletic great-grandfather, Col. Charles Glen Collins. Bill Laimbeer at six foot eleven is nationally famous for his outstanding basketball career with Notre Dame and the Detroit Pistons.

Collins and Amelia

Collins never saw his wife again and never beheld his only son, although it was apparent from his personal papers that he kept up with their lives from afar.

After the separation, Collins was remorseful and discouraged. His beloved sister Cornelia hurried from London to be with him and encouraged him to travel. Together they sailed to Naples, sojourning for ten days, thence to Scotland and finally sailed from Liverpool to Halifax. They vacationed in British Columbia, and then came to the States, and then Cornelia returned to Scotland.

Collins moved about the eastern states and became involved in numerous business ventures involving land developments, Texas oil ventures and other miscellaneous endeavors, and worked for a few years with W. H. Smith, a prominent engineer who built dams, racetracks, and other sizeable projects. Collins' work took him to Texas, California and South America raising funds for business ventures.

In 1914, he became involved with Amelia Wheeler, daughter of the founder of the Wheeler Sewing Machine Company, which was the biggest sewing machine manufacturer of the early 20th Century. It eventually merged with Singer.

Mr. Wheeler was not too impressed with the divorced Scotch playboy and would not consent to their marriage. However, this did not stop the impassioned couple, they eloped August 6, 1914, and Miss Wheeler became Collins' second spouse. They were just getting settled into married bliss when the "Great War" broke out in Europe, and England called for all out mobilization.

Although Collins had been out of the military for several years, was 34 years of age and a new bridegroom, he immediately booked passage for England to offer his services to do his part for his country.

His new bride went with him to England, but after two years of marriage to a warrior, she divorced him in 1916 but remained in England.

World War I & Gallipoli

When Collins landed at Liverpool in August 1914 after rushing from the States to offer his services for the war effort, he taxied directly from the train station to the war office in London. Hoping to be assigned to some unit that could take advantage of his combat experience, he was disappointed with his reception and his assignment for recruiting duty in London.

In September however, he bumped into his old friend from the African wars, Winston Churchill, who was now the First Lord of the Admiralty. Churchill told Collins that he was working on big war plans and was raising a division, a Royal Naval Division. Churchill asked, "Would you like to join us?" Collins could hardly hold back his excitement as he jumped at the offer.

He was made a lieutenant colonel and second in command of a regiment. The unit was quickly organized and trained hurriedly in the English countryside. In early October, the unit participated in an expedition of 10,000 troops to Antwerp to help the beleaguered Belgiums. The Germans reacted with overwhelming forces and chased them back with a force of 100,000. They returned to England, but the brief action was good for the inexperienced warriors.

Collins was promoted to commander of the Howe Battalion of the Royal Naval Division and trained for three more months in England. Among other officers assigned to the Howe was Arthur Asquith, son of the Prime Minister, and Rupert Brooke, a beloved poet of England whose works were favorably compared to Keats and Shelley.

Collins found that he desperately needed help in his command—an adjutant or second in command. His pleas through regular channels fell on deaf ears. Then he was inspired to call the Prime Minister's home and was immediately invited to luncheon. The fact that he was the commanding officer of their son probably didn't hurt.

At the luncheon, he pointed out his need for capable assistance in his command, and Margot, the famous wife of the Prime Minister, seemed keenly interested. She said that she thought she could get him some help. Margot stated, "I'll call General Barrow tomorrow."

A few days later, a telegram from the general arrived announcing the appointment of two officers to his regiment: Major John Sparling and Charles Kennedy Craufurd-Stuart. This was great news for Collins.

Sparling proved to be an able officer, but Craufurd-Stuart was another story—more later.

In February, Churchill called an urgent meeting of the commanders of the Royal Naval Division at Winston's Chesham Place house. He outlined a grandiose scheme, which had been approved by the war office, to send a major naval force into the Black

Sea through the Dardanelles Strait to attack the Turkish forts with naval bombardments. It was expected that the Turks would revolt against their government and change sides in the war, which would be a monumental step toward winning the war.

The RND would follow the Armada in troop ships and be used to occupy Constantinople and maintain order.

In February, the vast Armada sailed from England after an impressive send off by the King. The massive force sojourned at Malta for a few days, and the troops enjoyed a few days of leisure. In the smoking room of the *Royal George*, Collins and the young officers spent their evenings around a piano singing old favorites like, "Long Trail A Winding" and "Loch Lomond."

On March 18, the twenty-four-ship fleet steamed into the straits at daybreak and proceeded to bombard Turkish forts as they passed. The fleet included the most powerful battleship then afloat, the *Queen Elizabeth* and two first class cruisers the *Inflexible* and the *Invincible*.

The firing continued intensely from 7 a.m. for three hours, apparently successful as planned, but then at 10 o'clock, it was reported a French cruiser had been sunk with heavy loss of life. A torpedo or mine then struck the *Agamemnon*, and the *Ocean* was fatally struck and sank. Early in the afternoon, the *Inflexible* was hit a short distance from the *Queen Elizabeth*. This threw the naval commanders in turmoil for fear that the *Queen* would be next. The admiralty in London had repeatedly warned Admiral Derobeck not to needlessly endanger the battleship.

Shortly afterwards, the order to "Cease Fire" and "Break Off" were issued ending the naval campaign. Churchill's grand scheme was a dismal failure. Thereafter, the Royal Naval Division was sent to Egypt, ostensibly to guard the Suez Canal.

The high command had now decided on a land invasion of Turkey, and the infantry forces would await final plans in Egypt while Australian and New Zealand troops arrived and joined forces with them.

In mid-April, the entire expedition sailed to the Greek island of Skyros where a dress rehearsal of the invasion was staged. After the exercise, the young poet, Rupert Brooke, relaxed with his comrades, propped against an olive tree reciting verses from Homer's *Iliad*. On returning to his ship, he developed an acute case of "blood poisoning" probably from an insect bite, and his death that night would shock the British Empire. Collins took his pipers ashore and performed a ceremony beside the grave dug by torchlight while the pipers played the Scotch lament "Flowers of the Forest."

Brooke's sonnet, *The Soldier*, had been written only a year before.

"If I should die, think only this of me:
    That there's some corner of a foreign field
That is forever England. There shall be
    In that rich earth a richer dust concealed;
A dust whom England bore, shaped, made aware,
    Gave, once, her flowers to love, her ways to roam,
A body of England's, breathing English air,
    Washed by the rivers, blest by suns of home.

> And think, this heart, all evil shed away,
>   A pulse in the eternal mind, no less
>   Gives somewhere back the thought of England
>   given;
> Her sights and sounds; dreams happy as her day;
>   And laughter, learnt of friends; and gentleness,
>   In hearts at peace, under an English heaven.

The division later went ashore at Gallipoli and spent nine months of futile bloody trench warfare against the Turks who were well armed with German machine guns and protected by vast coils of barbed wire.

The climax of the campaign came on June 4, 1915, when an all out frontal assault was ordered. The attack on the entire front was set for high noon to be preceded by a naval bombardment for an hour and a half.

To the right of the RND were the French forces, which faced an up hill charge to the Turk trenches facing them on the heights above. When Collins' regiment was successful in finally breaching the Turk trenches in his sector, he discovered his fear was realized—the French had not been able to take their objective, and Turk machine guns fifty feet higher in elevation were turning towards the trenches now occupied by the British troops. This enfilade fire was murderous to the entrenched English. Collins ordered a hasty retreat back to their original position.

Collins looked back at his line and saw that the "Collinwood" battalion, which had been held in reserve, was being sent forward. After they had gotten within 300 yards of the Turk trenches, the machine guns opened up on them and wiped out ninety per cent of the 1,000 men in ten minutes.

Collins' outfit was suffering serious casualties also as they ran back towards their lines. Collins found a dry creek bed and crawled down it to return to their trenches. Only about 4 percent of his original attacking force got back to their trenches. When he got back, all he could do was nurse the wounded and give all a double ration of rum. The Howe Battalion had suffered 410 casualties; 14 officers and 279 men killed. The Collinwood Battalion suffered 900 casualties. In the one hour of the assault on June 4th at Gallopoli, the British lost more men than the entire British Army suffered in the Battle of Waterloo against Napoleon.

Prior to this battle, Major C.K. Craufurd-Stuart had been given command of the "Anson" Battalion. When Collins called over to him to discuss defense against a possible Turkish counter attack, he was puzzled when told he had not rejoined the unit prior to the assault.

Before the battle, Stuart had approached the regimental surgeon and asked to be treated for a slight wound where a bullet had grazed his cheek. The doctor told him to dab some iodine on it and forget it, but Stuart insisted on going back to the beaches for treatment and then insisted on going out to the hospital ship for medical help.

To top it off, an angry inquiry came to Collins headquarters from the division demanding to know how Major Stuart had been awarded the Distinguished Service Order without any recommendation from division. Collins disclaimed any knowledge of the matter. Later he learned from Arthur Asquith, that Stuart on his return to London had called on the Asquiths and audaciously gave them a detailed favorable account of his version of the bloody battle.

This was not the last that Collins heard from this gentleman.

Collins had brought his wife Amelia "Winkie" to England when he returned to volunteer for service. After Gallipoli, in May they separated for reasons unknown, and she later divorced him.

Thereafter, she married none other than Charles Kennedy-Craufurd-Stuart. As a footnote, during the early part of World War II, Stuart was living in Folkestone, England, when a mid-air explosion occurred over the Grove Cinema, and he was crushed to death.

Collins claimed that of all of the 96 commanding officers that had taken part in the landing at Gallipoli, he was the only one to be present both at the landing and the evacuation.

Col. Collins Fighting Extradition

After his return to England after Gallipoli, Collins was sent to an assignment at Christiana, Norway, working in intelligence ostensibly as a naval attaché. He then resigned his commission to work as a secret courier for high-level messages between the Allies and Russia to Peking and Yokohama agents.

In late September 1916, he went through Stockholm and Haparanda, Sweden, to get to Petrograd (St. Petersburg), Russia, where he made contact with Russian intelligence agents and was given top-secret packets to deliver to agents in Peking and in Yokohama. The Trans-Siberian Railroad got him to Peking, and from there, he reached Shanghai via the Yangtse River and then sailed to Yokohama where he completed his mission October 30th.

While in Yokohama, he was contacted by an old business acquaintance William H. Smith of St. Louis who excitedly told him about a huge oil deal he was working on. A Mr. Mitchell in Houston had a large oil field at Goose Creek that he urgently wanted to sell. Smith needed some help in swinging the deal. He felt he could sell it to a Shanghai firm, MacBain and Company, for a profit of some $300,000.

At this time, Collins was traveling with two rather wealthy ladies, Mrs. Olga Olsen, a widow, and her young friend, Elsie Benn-Muntz, wife of Sir Douglas Muntz and daughter of an English textile manufacturer, Harrison Benn. She was separated from her husband, had fallen in love with Collins, and was anxious to get a divorce in order to wed the glamorous Scot.

Smith, Collins and Mrs. Olsen joined together as a company to swing the oil deal. Smith was to get half the profits, and Collins and Mrs. Olsen were to split the other half.

Their negotiations with the MacBain firm were successful, and they felt the deal was all wrapped up. Smith had just come back from paying Mitchell $25,000 for an option to buy the field, and they celebrated their good fortune.

Smith headed back to Texas to close the deal, and Collins and his two happy companions moved along to visit India. At Bombay, the exuberant Collins wanted to please his new fiancé and took her to a couple of Bombay jewelers. He dazzled her with a diamond necklace at one shop, and at another, she was enthralled by a string of perfect pearls.

"What the heck?" thought Collins, "Easy come, easy go." The total cost of the jewelry was 4500 English pounds. He was able to give a valid cheque or draft for 1700 pounds. After the merchants checked out his credit favorably, they accepted his note for the balance.

By this time, the Russian Revolution had erupted, and the Trans-Siberian Railroad was closed. Collins abandoned all plans to go back to Petrograd.

Collins and his bride-to-be, along with her "chaperone" Mrs. Olsen, headed gaily back to the States. Collins had to return to Canada at Valcartier where he was to be in charge of training Canadian troops. The girls were to travel about a bit, and then join him later for more fun and games. Unfortunately, the sky fell on Collins when his friend W.H. Smith contacted him and gave the gloomy news that Mitchell had sold the oil field to someone else, in spite of their option. So much for the big bucks! He recalled the losing hand in Baccarat that cost him a quarter million back in 1904, but this one hurt even more. What could he do about the jewelry note? He already had a bankruptcy hanging over him back in England.

He quickly left for Texas to see what could be done about the deal. Going by way of Washington, he stopped to confer with a top law firm, Bartlett and Poe, not just about the oil deal, but what was he to expect from the Indian merchants.

After visiting Houston and getting the bad news confirmed on the sale of the oil field, he took the train back to New Orleans and checked in to the Grunewald Hotel (now the Roosevelt). After visiting the Boston Club for dinner, he was rudely accosted at the hotel by a local law officer who put him under arrest on charges of criminal fraud filed by the two Indian merchants. Taken to the House of Detention, he was thrown in with drunks, vagrants and criminals awaiting trial. He was not a happy camper. It was November 4, 1917, and the low point of his life.

Collins pondered his past as he tried to sleep on the filthy mattress, surrounded by the snoring and bellowing and smells of the dregs of society. At age 27, he had had more advantages than most—born to a prominent wealthy family always anxious to help; and had had more rewarding experiences than most—participated in three successful combat campaigns; had had sudden wealth thrust upon him several times, only to immediately squander every time; had won the heart of his only true love only to lose her and his only son from his own foolish actions; had stupidly turned down his family's offer to rescue him financially from an idiotic fiasco of his own making; had thrown away on one hand of cards a quarter million dollars which could have bailed him out of his bankruptcy—oh, so many stupid mistakes!

Collins contacted his Washington attorneys. They advised him to get a local lawyer to get bailed out. He hired J. Zack Spearing who quickly got him released on $2,000 bail.

Then there began a long journey through the labyrinth of federal court proceedings. The British government was seeking to extradite him to return to India to face trial. The charges were criminal charges, not just a suit to collect the debt, and in India at that time, the penalty could be death.

However, Collins believed, even a sentence of a few years in an Indian prison would probably mean death anyway. Consequently, he was determined to fight extradition at all costs.

The wheels of justice ground slowly and a hearing was held on his attorneys' motion to dismiss the extradition petition, then appealed, then reheard, then appealed again. The process would continue for over five years, including three trips to the U. S. Supreme Court.

Shortly after his arrest, Elsie came to comfort him and married him in the prison March 12, 1918. However, as his ordeal continued with his being in and out of jail constantly between hearings, Elsie's passion began to cool. When his second appeal to the Supreme Court was rejected in November 1919 and it appeared that he would have to remain confined indefinitely, Elsie left for New York and England.

However, in early 1920, Collins was able to get help from John W. McGrath and another gentleman whom he had met in the Boston Club. They guaranteed a $25,000 bond, which gained his freedom for the remainder of the appeal procedures.

Thereafter Collins was free to come and go as he pleased. He got an apartment in the French Quarter and became quite a man about town. He made many friends in New Orleans society, becoming quite a favored guest for St. Charles Avenue and garden district parties. He also was warmly received in the literary set, which included Sherwood Anderson, renown author of the day; William Spratling, a potter of note whose life was later made into a movie, and William Faulkner, a young writer who had one novel to his credit.

Faulkner was rooming with Spratling on Pirate Alley beside the St. Louis Cathedral in a small house that today is The Faulkner Book Store.

Collins continued his interest in gambling and horse racing and knew a number of owners who raced at the Fairgrounds. One day he got lucky or perhaps had a tip on a sure thing and won $100,000 at the track. He immediately bought a yacht, *Josephine*, docked at Lake Ponchatrain. He gratefully shared his good fortune with his jailers and took them on an extended cruise on the lake.

The most significant cruise taken however was one for the entire literary crowd, including Faulkner. For three days, they cruised the lake, once running aground near the north shore. Faulkner got restless after hours of being stuck in the mud and enticed a young lass on the boat to go with him in the yacht's dingy to shore. They sought to reach Mandeville through the swamp for they had heard it was a swinging town with great bars and music. However, the swamp was too much for them, particularly from the mosquitoes, and they abandoned their quest and got a fisherman to take them back to the yacht.

The cruise is immortalized by Faulkner's second novel, Mosquitoes, wherein Col. Collins is portrayed by the character Major Ayers.

The Times Picayune later reported in Collins' obituary:

> "Colonel Collins took to the old House of Detention the most magnificent wardrobe the inmates ever saw. He and his jailers spent afternoons sailing on his yacht. Turnkeys were his messengers to his bookmaker, carrying his money, making his bets on horse races at various tracks.
> Then Colonel Collins wearied of this confinement. He arranged for an escape. He took the key of his cell with him as a souvenir. But he was captured on the New Orleans waterfront, and taken back to the House of Detention, just as he was about to board a freighter for London."

Col. Collins—The Last Years

After nearly six years of fighting extradition to India, Lt. Col. Charles Glen Collins lost his final appeal to the U.S. Supreme Court. He sailed for England June 13, 1923, in custody of Inspector George Miles of Scotland Yard. After an attempt to appeal to his old friend, King George V, was unsuccessful, he sailed to Bombay. Denied bail, Collins had to endure an Indian jail cell until his first trial on December 2nd.

With Collins and his attorneys and his family pulling every string conceivable, he managed to get a jury of half Britishers and half natives. A deposition from his friend, W. H. Smith, was accepted into evidence and corroborated Collins' story of the oil deal that went sour and prevented him from having funds to pay for the jewelry as planned. His war record and his family background gave him credibility before the jury, and he was acquitted December 10th.

He had to endure a second trial on a charge from the other merchant, but again he was acquitted February 12, 1924.

The heavy burden he had borne for six years was finally lifted. He took a leisurely voyage back, via Shanghai, Singapore and Hong Kong, sailed to Seattle and arrived back in New Orleans on April 2nd to the joyous welcome of his friends and generous news stories in the New Orleans papers.

Collins' wife, Elsie Benn-Muntz Collins, had fled from him when he had to spend a lot of time in confinement, and Collins filed suit for divorce on grounds of adultery. She had returned to Europe, and when she received the divorce summons, she answered his charges of adultery by casually admitting in glowing detail her living with Captain Eric Mc Gunning in London as man and wife, providing details of their life.

Her paramour was also being sued by his spouse for "restitution of conjugal rights," and Elsie curiously detailed what she was wearing when Gunning was served with his papers, "I was wearing a silk jacket and silk Persian trousers." This is perhaps an indication of her "devil may care" attitude. Collins was granted his divorce, but it did not become final until August 1926.

During Collins' long stay in the Crescent City, he had become very close to Mr. and Mrs. John W. McGrath. Mr. McGrath had founded a large department store chain centered in Brookhaven, Mississippi, but lived in New Orleans. His son, Jay McGrath, ran the department store business. After Mr. McGrath died in October 1922 Collins and Mrs. McGrath married five years later. They were apparently a good match, although she was eight years older.

Collins had established a rice brokerage business with offices on Decatur Street, known as "Rice 'O Lay." When he and Mrs. McGrath married, he sold Rice O' Lay and concentrated on real estate, buying rental properties in the Garden District and renovating or remodeling them.

When the Depression struck, the fortunes of the new couple were hit rather hard. Property was difficult to rent, and rent hard to collect and taxes were severe. Mrs. Collins' fortune in securities suffered greatly as the stock market plummeted.

The couple decided they could do better moving to Brookhaven where her son, Jay, operated McGrath's Department Store. Col. and Mrs. Collins moved in with Mr. and Mrs. Jay McGrath in an upstairs apartment in the old Butterfield home on Storm Avenue.

Collins' family helped him out. On a trip to Scotland with his new bride, Collins mother gave him three thousand dollars, which was sufficient for the couple to buy a fine old residence at the depression era prices. Later Collins' brothers sent him a small monthly check.

The Colonel became active in the community life of the small town. He wrote a weekly column for the semi-weekly <u>Leader</u> under the pseudonym "Sancho Panza." He joined with other golfers in working to construct a golf course. Until a course was built, the golfers would go to a pasture of a friendly farmer and create a makeshift course. Later with the aid of the WPA, a nine-hole course was constructed at the site of the present country club.

Collins had never been around small children before, and when he joined the McGrath family, he became enthralled with the shy, charming little pre-schooler, Jayne McGrath, daughter of Mr. & Mrs. Jay McGrath. He would do anything she wanted. Collins could not abide any discipline that her parents meted out, no matter how merited it was.

Once after Jayne was sentenced to some harsh punishment, such as a light switching, Collins secretly told his pet "granddaughter" that he was not going to put up with such cruel and unusual punishment, that he was taking her right away to New Orleans where she could live happily. The two got in the Colonel's Cadillac and headed south. When Jayne's father learned of the escape, he called the authorities and had the police at Magnolia thirty miles south to put up a roadblock and capture the fugitives. This was easily accomplished without incident, and Collins meekly returned to Brookhaven. How far he would have taken the caper no one knows.

Collins had time on his hands in Brookhaven. He was not the type to be idle. He began writing his memoirs. His early life and career as a soldier in the Sudan and Boer conflicts were fully covered. The Gallipoli campaign was written as though it were fiction, and he was depicted as "Colen Glendon," but all other characters were real people, i.e. Winston Churchill, Sir Kitchener, Ian Hamilton, and Charles Kennedy- Craufurd-Stuart.

TIMEOUT: Craufurd-Stuart is an involved story also. He is the captain despised by Collins for his apparent cowardice at Gallipoli and for then obtaining a medal by deceit. Collins' feelings toward him weren't helped when Stuart married Collins' estranged second wife, "Winkie." Then, in 1918, he was the subject of a scandal in Washington when he secretly accused a female worker of spying for the Germans. A tap was put on her telephone and although nothing incriminating to her was found, there were some juicy conversations between her and her illicit lover, none other than Bernard Baruch. Later Stuart, as an aide to the British ambassador, thoughtlessly made an insulting remark at a party about President Wilson, which was reported to the President. Wilson demanded that Stuart be recalled as a persona-non-gratis, but the British ambassador would not do so. This came in the midst of the negotiations over the establishment of the League of Nations. The bitterness over this escalated and helped result in the failure of the United States to join the League. Later authorities researching Craufurd-Stuart suspected that during WWI he had been an agent for British Intelligence, which might explain that he was ordered to avoid the murderous charge at Gallipoli in order to keep him alive as an agent. It has never been proved. **NOW BACK TO COL. COLLINS:**

He also wrote an account of a swindle perpetrated on him and another by a Mrs. Studebaker, a widow of one of the Studebaker brothers.

However, the creation in which he took most pride was the account of Gallipoli. He dearly wanted to get it published. A call was made to his old friend, William Faulkner, in Oxford, inviting him to come to Brookhaven for a weekend—he had something for him to read.

Faulkner, who really enjoyed the company of the Scot, accepted and came down on the train. The McGraths entertained the great writer with a sumptuous dinner, wine and conversation. As Faulkner prepared to retire to his room for the evening, Collins thrust upon him the manuscript of Gallipoli. He said, "Bill, scan this over tonight and let me know what you think of it in the morning."

At breakfast, an extra fine meal was laid out. Collins had urged the ladies of the house to go all out. After the juice, eggs, sausage, bacon, etc, and finally the cup of fine, strong coffee, the conversation had covered everything from the depression to Roosevelt, the price of cotton, Ole Miss football, and the latest movies, but not one word about the manuscript. Collins could stand it no longer. He said, "Damn it Bill, what did you think about the manuscript?"

Faulkner thoughtfully put down his coffee and took a slow draw from his pipe. With great restraint, he earnestly looked at Collins, "Charlie, if it weren't about you, would you read it?" and then returned to his pipe.

Collins never attempted to publish the book.

To the end, Collins was financially crippled by his early life mistakes. He had been thrown into bankruptcy as a result of the cosigning of the many notes for Innis Kerr. His inheritances from his grandmother, mother, and an aunt were all fought over by the bankruptcy trustees. In the last year of his life, he was still desperately trying to get a share of these estates, but without success.

Collins was a typical Britisher who had a deep lifetime respect and love for his kings and queens. When his old friend, King George V, died, he promoted a simultaneous commemorative service at the Brookhaven Episcopal Church, timed to coincide with the services in England. The Colonel made a moving tribute to the deceased sovereign. Afterwards, he sent the widow, Queen Mary, a clipping of the newspaper account and a kind letter of condolence. Apparently, he had no ill will from the King's failure to help him in his troubles earlier in India.

A reply from Marlborough House arrived two weeks later.

"MARLBOROUGH HOUSE

PRIVATE   S.W.I.

Aug. 17th 1937

Dear Colonel Collins,

I have had the honour of submitting to Queen Mary your letter of August 6th, together with its enclosures.

In reply I am commanded to convey to you an expression of Queen Mary's warm thanks for your letter & photograph, together with the cutting, which Her Majesty has read with much interest. The words spoken by you on the occasion of the Memorial Service for His Late Majesty King George V greatly touched The Queen and Her

Robert E. Jones

Majesty thinks the wording on the Memorial Tablet in the American Episcopal Church at Brookhaven very charming.

I am to assure you that Queen Mary much appreciates your kind thought in sending the particulars of this Memorial Service for her information.

Her Majesty does hope that you found your mother's health better than you anticipated.

> *Believe me,*
> *Yours very truly,*
> *Gerald Chichester*
> *Private Secretary"*

One year later, Collins developed lung cancer, which worsened rapidly. He was sent to the Vicksburg Sanatorium and continued to write his column as long as possible. When his physicians informed him there was no more hope, he commented, "Life owes me nothing. I have tasted all of its joys." He died quietly in his sleep September 21, 1939, and is buried in Rose Hill Cemetery in Brookhaven. He was 59 years old.

GRIERSON'S RAID

In early 1863, when General Grant was gathering his forces for the all out Vicksburg campaign, he sent Colonel B. H. Grierson on a daring mission through the heart of Mississippi.

On April 17th, Colonel Grierson embarked from LaGrange, Tennessee, leading 1700 crack Union cavalrymen from Illinois and Iowa on the spectacular raid through central and southwestern Mississippi.

The goal was to draw Rebel forces away from the Vicksburg area and to wreak as much havoc to railroads, telegraph facilities and confederate supplies as possible.

By April 26th, Grierson had reached Raleigh, capturing the local sheriff and relieving him of some three thousand dollars of Confederate currency.

Grierson then headed southwest and crossed the Pearl River near Georgetown, utilizing in part the ferry after convincing the ferryman that they were Rebels. After weeks on the raid, the cavalrymen's uniforms were dirty, muddy, and were not easily identifiable as Union troops. Most local citizens, having never seen Cavalry before, assumed them to be Confederate forces.

They headed straight for the New Orleans, Jackson and Great Northern Railroad, striking it at Hazlehurst, tearing up tracks, destroying cars and a large amount of shells and supplies destined for

Grand Gulf and Port Gibson. As usual, there were brave citizens offering to oppose the Yanks, but as in every such incident, the futility of opposing the well armed and trained cavalry by old men and boys with shotguns and old rifles quickly became apparent and no one was killed or wounded.

Grierson hit Gallatin and then headed west to join the main U.S. forces in the Vicksburg area. However, upon reaching Union Church, he encountered Mississippi's Colonel Wirt Adams's forces and sporadic firing occurred between them.

Grierson camped about two miles north of Union Church on the Snyder Plantation for the night. The Colonel deliberately let a captured local citizen overhear that he planned to march towards Natchez and Fayette in the morning and then released the prisoner.

Colonel Adams received this false information and prepared a mammoth ambush for Grierson west of Union Church. However, the Yankee commander headed southeast towards Brookhaven to again attack the railroad.

As the troops rode toward Brookhaven on the morning of April 29th, they encountered many frightened civilians carrying their most precious belongings on their wagons to escape the Yankee threat, which they expected was impending from Hazlehurst. Many of the refugees frantically warned the Grierson troopers to beware because the Yankees were headed for Brookhaven.

Upon reaching the outskirts of Brookhaven, there were about 500 courageous local older men and boys, armed with their hunting weapons ready to defend their home. After a few shots taken at a distance, they quickly withdrew from the field of battle as the well mounted cavalry troops charged into town at full gallop with sabers flashing. About 200 locals were taken prisoner temporarily. The raiders burned the depot and all rail cars they could find and tore up some of the rails and destroyed the telegraph facility.

Grierson and his officers then retired to the local hotel for a good meal. The owner, frightened at first, calmed down and served them well with a liberal compensation from the Confederate funds taken from the Raleigh sheriff.

The proprietor bade the officers good bye saying he "wished the Yanks would come every day, if they paid like you 'uns do."

Other than the depot and railroad facilities destroyed, there was no other destruction of property in the town, nor any harming of local civilians. Outside of town, the Yanks found the Rebel training camp with several hundred tents, and considerable supplies, ammunition and arms, all of which were destroyed.

Before leaving town, all prisoners were paroled as Grierson headed south and camped for the night on the Gill Plantation about 8 miles south of Brookhaven.

The next day he attacked the rail facilities at Bogue Chitto, destroying bridges and trestles approaching the town, burning the depot and 15 freight cars and capturing a very large "secession flag."

They continued on to Summit, doing their thing to the railroad and telegraph, but during their exploring around the town, some of the men discovered hidden under a long board sidewalk some forty barrels of Louisiana rum! But before they could transfer much of it to their canteens, the Colonel found out about it and, as a true killjoy, ordered all to empty their canteens and refill them with spring water, and furthermore, to smash all the barrels and to get back in the saddle to leave. In an ultimate test of their discipline, the men meekly obeyed, slowly saluting and soberly salivating, while the men of the town looked on in shock, weeping and cursing the Yanks for this heartless unforgivable atrocity.

Colonel Grierson rode proudly out with head held high, but with mixed emotions. No one had checked his canteen.

Ending the famous raid, Grierson's force paraded into Baton Rouge at 11:00 on May 2nd to rejoin Grant's army. They had lost only 3 killed and 7 wounded after raiding for over two weeks and some 500 miles through the heart of enemy territory.

Although he did major damage to transportation and communication facilities and to stores of Rebel arms and supplies, he left every community without any deliberate harm to civilians and their homes, farms and businesses. He gained the respect of the enemy as a gentlemen and a chivalrous officer.

THE HOBO HEROES

In the late hot summer of 1932, two Brookhaven teenagers were riding a freight train westward from Pensacola along the Mississippi gulf coast. Larry Williamson and John David Kees had just finished one month's civilian military training corps (a depression era program for young men) at Ft. Barranca, Florida, and had each been given fifteen dollars cash for expenses home. However, for teenagers in the depth of the great depression, that much cash had rarely been seen before; and they eagerly chose to save the money and ride the freight trains home.

As they lazily lounged on the hard floor of a bumpy boxcar, gazing out the open doorway, they passed the impressive buildings of the Gulf Coast Military Academy, then a prestigious private military grade and high school in Gulfport. John David said to his pal, "That's where the rich boys go, so I guess we'll never get there." Larry tacitly agreed as they spotted some of the smartly uniformed students on the campus as the train moved out of sight of the school.

Some sixty years later these same boys, now retired naval officers in their mid seventies, were sitting on a bench at the Naval Home at Gulfport where they resided. Larry remembered John David's remark of decades past and said, "Well, you were wrong after all. Here we are." The Navy had acquired the old school property and had constructed an elegant ten-story facility for Naval retirees on

Robert E. Jones

the exact site of the old academy. John David knew exactly what he was talking about. "Yeah," he said, "but it took a while, didn't it!"

A lot had happened in the interim. Since a young lad, Larry had been fascinated with aviation. He had spent as much time as he could around the old "Ulmer Field" in Brookhaven. It wasn't much more than a fairly level pasture alongside the railroad but did have a tall flashing beacon and a hangar of sorts. Larry was enthralled by the barnstorming pilots who occasionally came to thrill audiences with acrobatics and offer rides in the primitive biplanes of the time for a modest fee.

Larry envisioned a more exciting and fulfilling career than pumping gas at the Hog Chain country store. His father had bought 3 acres in the forks of the road in 1927 from J.M. Summers and had established a little country store and made a deal with The Texas Company for selling their gas, for which he got $25 per month and a small commission. After his father died in 1930, Larry and his brothers helped his stepmother run the store, but Larry's heart was in the sky. After graduating from Brookhaven High School in 1933, he knew he had to strike out on his own, particularly since his stepmother was going to remarry, and there would not be enough room for him at home.

He was finally able to get in the U.S. Navy in 1935, went to Norfolk for boot camp, and later got assigned to the aircraft carrier, *Saratoga*, commanded by Admiral Bull Halsey. Larry was in Hog Chain heaven; well, almost, since he was not yet a flyer.

Admiral Halsey took a liking to the young Mississippian and assigned him to the bridge of the ship where he became the "voice of Halsey," that is, he had the job of announcing on the ship's speaker, "NOW HEAR THIS, ALL HANDS, etc." - - - Halsey liked his baritone voice and the slow Mississippi drawl.

In 1937, Larry finally got his wish to go to flight training at Pensacola, and after almost flunking out, gained his wings. He went on to become a pilot of a big PBY, the flying boat of the Navy used primarily for ocean reconnaissance and search and rescue operations.

Meanwhile, Larry's old football teammate and friend, John David, was finishing LSU where he had made ends meet by playing in a dance band, which had gotten so successful that he had to take a big cut in income when he got a New Orleans bank job after graduation.

After fighting the battle of numbers in the bank for a few years, John David also wanted a more glamorous career and enlisted in the Navy in 1940. After his training was complete, he was thrilled to get a highly coveted assignment to Hawaii at the big base at Pearl Harbor.

PEARL HARBOR

On that famous day of infamy, December 7, 1941, John David was awakened in his quarters by unusual plane noises and what sounded like bombs, machine guns and anti aircraft fire. Leaping from his bed, he hurriedly dressed and rushed towards his place of duty on the other side of the bay. Dashing through machine gun bullets and shell fragments, he reached the bay and got on a launch to cross to his place of duty. After delays for picking up wounded men and delivering them to medical help, John David arrived at his post to find it in flames and shambles. A week later when the smoke was beginning to abate, he was awaiting in line at the post office to mail letters home when he thought he saw something familiar with the back of the head of a man in front of him. Peering closer, he saw it was his old hobo classmate, Hog Chain Larry. They had a great reunion, recalling old times over a few adult beverages, but had to part again as duty called them to separate ways.

Larry was sent to a base in the New Hebrides and was very active in his PBY as the early Pacific naval battles began and the crucial struggle over the island of Guadalcanal ensued. He patrolled the South Pacific area reporting on Japanese vessels.

THE *JUNEAU*

At this time, one of a new class of cruisers was active in the area. It was the *Juneau*, with its complement of 700 men. The new cruiser was lightly armored, designed for speed and mobility and intended for anti-aircraft support for aircraft carriers.

Among the *Juneau's* crew were the five "fighting Sullivan brothers," who became probably the most famous family group of World War II particularly after a movie was made to commemorate them.

Mississippi Gumbo

The ship had been engaged in the Battle of Santa Cruz in mid-October and had been badly damaged and was limping along in convoy with several other naval vessel, trying to get back to port for repairs.

Friday the 13th of November 1942 was not a lucky day for the ship. Japanese warships had come upon them in the dark and suddenly turned intense searchlights on the *Juneau* and the other U.S. ships. An all night gun battle followed. The *Juneau* was so close to the Jap ships they could see the faces of the enemy sailors near the searchlights running about. Shortly, a shell hit amidships of the *Juneau*, and then a torpedo from a submarine hit the rear portion containing the ships magazine. The explosion of the torpedo was followed immediately by the detonation of the explosives in the ship's magazine. The central portion of the ship was disintegrated—the bow and stern sections were completely separated and sank within 20 seconds.

Of the 700 human beings on the *Juneau*, about 150 who were on deck were able to survive the immediate disaster, thrown into the oil-covered sea; however, bleeding wounds and vicious sharks rapidly reduced the number of survivors to a handful in rafts. One of the Sullivans, George, had survived relatively unhurt and was seen swimming from raft to raft desperately wiping oil from sailors' faces futilely trying to find any of his brothers.

The other ships in the convoy fled the scene and did not return to search for survivors (1) because of the danger of the enemy subs and (2) a belief that because of the catastrophic explosion they witnessed, there were not likely to be any survivors.

However, the survivors in the three rafts were spotted by a B-17 pilot shortly after the *Juneau's* sinking, but he was under orders not to break radio silence and waited until his return to base to report it. The Navy, its hands full with continuing engagements with the Japanese, failed to initiate any serious rescue effort until Admiral Halsey learned of the existence of the survivors three days later. In fact, due to snafus in communication, Halsey had not even been informed of *Juneau's* sinking; and when told there was no concerted rescue effort in progress, he blew his stack.

Immediately, the destroyer, *USS Meade*, was sent to search the area; but found nothing, returned to base, and reported no sighting.

Finally, on the 18th, a PBY was sent to search the area; and the *USS Ballard* was also dispatched to the area. The PBY found them and was ordered to circle, keeping them in sight until the *Ballard* got there to pick them up. However, darkness came and there was no sign of the *Ballard*, so the PBY had to return to base.

The survivors were desperately in need of help. They had no water or food, and several were wounded. Only twelve remained alive. Three of the strongest had left the others, paddling for a distance island.

At daybreak, Lt. Williamson was sent in his PBY to search. After vainly searching all morning and into the afternoon, he reluctantly started to return to base. Then—there they were! Three rafts with men aboard—he couldn't ascertain how many live ones there were—but some were fit enough to stand and feebly wave to the plane.

He was ordered to stay and keep the rafts in sight and guide the *Ballard*, which was headed for the site.

Circling above the pitiful rafts for about an hour Williamson assessed the situation: Limited remaining daylight; fuel getting low; rough sea and wind; the near death condition of the surviving sailors in the rafts; and the strong possibility that if he stayed until dark, the rescue ship probably would not find them in time.

Weighing all the factors, Williamson called to ask permission to land and try to pick up the survivors. After some delay, he was told to "Use your own discretion." His discretion was to do all he could within reason, even though at great risk, to try to save the desperate sailors. Williamson had never landed in open ocean before—always on calm bay waters. The sea was a little angry, a 14 knot wind and swells of five to six feet. "Hang on, we're going in," he announced over the intercom. The men's confidence in Larry overrode their fear, and they nervously joked while some crossed themselves as they headed in.

Williamson eased down on the throttle for a full stall landing. The plane dropped sharply and made a hard landing, "cracking a bunch of rivets" as he later described it.

Maneuvering to get to the closest raft was difficult. As the plane taxied toward the raft, the survivors were paddling furiously to come to the plane's forward "blister," and it became apparent that they were about to collide with the propeller of the port engine. Three times Larry had to back off to avoid a disaster. The plane was bouncing up and down with the swells, and the prop was hitting the water on the down movements. Finally one of the crew climbed out on the wing and got a line to the raft and pulled them beside the plane's float and was unable to get all five of the men into the plane.

By that time, it was almost dark. In all the maneuvering to get the first group boarded, they had gotten disoriented; and the other rafts were nowhere to be seen. Time and fuel were at a critical level, so Williamson opted to take off with what he had and to come back the next morning if the *USS Ballard* did not find the rafts.

Taking off was not a simple matter in view of the waves, but using full power the plane, which was light due to the low fuel and having no bombs or depth charges aboard, was able to get airborne. As he reached about 100 feet elevation, he spotted another raft with one man aboard. He signaled encouragement to him but had to go on. The five weak survivors were delivered to medical personnel as soon as the plane got to the base.

Before he started to return in the early morning, he learned that the *USS Ballard* had picked up the other survivors.

In all, ten men were rescued: five by Williamson; two by the *USS Ballard* and three had made it to an island safely.

The navy was not proud of its role in the aftermath of the *Juneau's* sinking, and the only recognition given to any survivors or their rescuers was the Legion of Merit awarded to the three survivors who made it to the island on their own strength.

ALASKA PROCLAMATION

In 1987 the Alaska Legislature passes a resolution which stated in part as follows: "On the seventh day, a PBY patrol plane piloted by Lieutenant Williamson spotted some of the survivors. Seas were rough and in landing his plane to rescue the few *USS JUNEAU* survivors, Lieutenant Williamson put himself, his crew and the safety of his plane on the line. Because of his heroic effort, this marked the end of suffering and anguish for those in the water. His rescue saved one-half of the *USS JUNEAU* survivors. Out of 700 men only 10 survived the *USS JUNEAU* tragedy."

JOHN DAVID'S CAREER

After Pearl Harbor, John David, who also was a naval aviator, completed two years of Pacific duty and then was reassigned to Brazil to fly anti-submarine patrol in the Atlantic and the Caribbean. He later served throughout the Korean conflict on the aircraft career, *Princeton.*

After retiring in 1962 he was able to pursue his passion for the theater in New York City, and studied acting and directing at Columbia University, earning a master's degree in that field.

His professional acting career took him to many theaters across the country as well as before the bright lights of the New York stage.

In his last performance in the "Big Apple," he played the role of "Doc" in Tennessee Williams' "Small Craft Warning." Mr. Williams who was in attendance at the performances especially liked the "Doc" character he had created and would frequently add or change his lines, sometimes only minutes before the curtain. He was persuaded to try his hand at acting and began to alternate nightly with John David in the role, coached and directed by Kees. The great playwright, though nervous, immensely enjoyed the experience, but avowed it was not only his first role in a play, but also his last.

In 1991, John David took up residence in the plush Naval home in Gulfport. He pulled as many strings as he could to help get his old buddy Williamson to join him there, at the spot they had chugged past on the freight train sixty years before. However, Williamson stayed there only a few years and then gave in to the pleas of his daughter and moved to Texas where he resided with her family, but now lives in Sacramento, California.

SWEET PEA TO THE RESCUE

Janine "Sweet Pea" Adams, widow of Versie Adams, who was born Janine Dardenne, has reason to vividly remember her teenage years in Belgium during World War II. She lived in the little village of Boirs, 10 miles west of Liege and about 40 miles north of Bastogne.

Although Germany had been at war with England and France since September 1939, Belgium was nervously sitting on the sidelines until May 10, 1940, when the German juggernaut blitzed into Holland and Belgium in a move to by-pass the French Maginot line.

The first notice of the invasion to Boirs was an old man marching down the village street at 5 a.m. on May 10, beating on an old washtub like a bass drum and hollering "It's War! It's War!" and the sounds of bombs and Stuka dive bombers shrieking in the East.

The nearby fortress of Eben-Emael close to the German border was easily by-passed by the German panzer divisions, as they headed for an end run into France.

The village was not destroyed but bombs killed about five people and a few cows.

The surrender of Belgium and France came quickly and by mid June 1940, the fighting was over…temporarily.

But by 1943 after Britain had regained its strength and America was active as her ally, the war heated up again in Western Europe, at least in the air.

On the evening of August 17, 1943, in the house of Joseph Godin, a railroad conductor, there was a tense clandestine meeting. The guest of honor was Joseph Walters of Pittsburgh, Pennsylvania, who had been extricated from an apple tree near the village. He had parachuted from his stricken B-17 which had been attacked by German fighter planes while on its way back from a bombing raid on the ball bearing factories of Schweinfurt, Germany. Some workers from a nearby box factory had helped him get untangled from his chute and the tree.

They had been able to communicate with him only to the extent of asking him if he wanted to surrender to the Germans. In spite of a language barrier he made it clear that he did not want to surrender.

He was given a glass of brandy and then hidden under crates in the box factory until the Belgians felt that it was safe to move him to the house in the village.

At the house, still in his flight uniform, nursing a broken forearm, scratched and fearful, but boosted somewhat by the brandy, he tried to communicate with his rescuers, but he spoke no French and they spoke no English. Hastily they sent for Janine Dardenne, a fifteen-year-old lass who was taking an English course in her school.

Finally into the kitchen came Janine Dardenne who possessed the priceless knowledge of a little English, accompanied by her worried mother, who had brought along her knitting as a distraction if stopped by the Germans.

Sergeant Walters stood up as the mother and daughter entered, a courtesy not normally observed by the villagers. "Say something to him in English," the group urged Jeanine.

Hastily trying to recall something appropriate she could only come up momentarily with a phrase the schoolgirls repeated frequently.

"MAY I KISS YOU?" she blurted out to the startled American. This unexpected request expelled the pressure packed atmosphere and after a stunned pause brought a welcome burst of laughter and a broad grin from Joe. He leaned forward across the table and allowed Janine to plant a smack on his cheek to the perplexity of the puzzled non-English speakers present.

"Tell him he will stay with Joseph Godin tonight. Tomorrow he will go in a truck to Liege," where he will stay a few days." "Tell him we will make all the arrangement."

The villagers coordinating with the "Resistance" or "underground" were able to get ID papers for Walters and started him on a long journey, sometimes by truck, sometimes by wagon and a lot of times by walking through Belgium and into France.

He would stay periodically for days at a time with farmers or others along the trip. For about three weeks, he stayed with a doctor in Liege, who treated his broken arm and helped him regain his strength. Shortly after he left, however, the brave doctor was interrogated by the Germans and shot for aiding the enemy.

On each leg of the trip, he was accompanied by a different native guide who would do all the talking when encountered by others.

Eventually Walters made it across the Pyrenees into Spain and finally Gibraltar from where he was flown back to England, arriving shortly before Christmas, 1943.

A prearranged signal was broadcast over the BBC for the benefit of the brave Belgians. "The Rabbit is back in the hutch" which brought great celebration to the village of Boirs.

The most agonizing experience that Janine endured during the whole war had nothing to do with hunger or physical danger, but was not being able to tell her best friend and others about her exciting role in helping the American airman and having actually kissed him! Her father had forcefully demanded that she could not tell <u>anyone</u> about the event, for all the people involved could be killed for their role. So, her tongue probably still has scars from biting it in order not to tell.

<u>D-DAY</u>

Throughout the war, food was a constant problem in the village. Whenever a rumor was heard about a shop somewhere that had bread for sale, people would rush to it with their ration stamps.

On June 5, 1944, such a report was received about a shop a few miles west of the village. Janine set out on her bicycle early the next morning to get some bread, but on the way, she caught up with a column of German soldiers marching westwardly. Unable to pass through the column she tagged along behind, irked that she would be delayed on her mission.

She soon noticed an airplane diving down towards them and when the troops suddenly panicked and dove for the ditches, she realized it was an American plane, and she hurriedly joined the Germans in the ditch as the plane sprayed the road with machine gun fire. Fortunately, she was unhurt but decided to return home, breadless and breathless.

Back at the village she learned that the allies had landed at Normandy—The Invasion had come at last! Joy reigned in the village; a few long-hidden bottles of brandy and wine were brought out for the celebration.

By September, the Germans had pulled back and left the village between the two armies. Janine and other youngsters would climb up in the village church tower to watch the road to the west for signs of approaching allies. The sound of the war was all around and above them as artillery and aircraft action was constant.

Finally, Janine spotted a curious looking vehicle approaching the village. Not knowing who or what it was, she shouted to the village that something was coming. It was soon identified as an American jeep with two Americans in it. The village went wild. More long -hidden bottles of brandy and wine were produced. The soldiers were toasted, kissed, hugged, and made to drink from everybody's bottles until they finally insisted that they be allowed to proceed before they got too intoxicated.

BATTLE OF THE BULGE

When winter came, it came with a vengeance. It was the bitterest cold within memory in mid December. The joy of seeming victory turned sour when the Germans launched their mammoth counter-offensive and once again, Boirs was between the warring armies.

The allies were being pushed back largely as a result of miserable weather conditions which kept all allied warplanes on the ground. However, after General Patton made his famous prayer to God for a break in the weather, it happened. The weather cleared up and suddenly the air was filled with the drone of thousands of allied planes of all types flying over going to the rescue and support of the stagnated troop positions. The sound of the warplanes was so intense over the village that the buildings and ground vibrated and no other sounds could be heard. The relief that this development brought to the village was enormous. Many dropped to their knees in grateful prayer.

The war soon moved on away from Boirs, deep into Germany and life improved somewhat as American troops were prominent in the area.

Janine got a job right after VE Day as an interpreter for an American ordnance depot, working with a Mississippi staff sergeant, Versie Adams. At first, neither liked the other, but it wasn't long before civility turned to friendship, then friendship to romance and finally marriage on December 22, 1945.

Janine was allowed to come to the states in April 1946, some four months before her husband. She lived with his parents in Brookhaven while he lived with hers in Boirs, but finally in August, they were united and, as they say, the rest is history.

Oh, yes, she was able to locate Joe Walters in Pittsburgh in 1996 and has talked to him many times since. He visited Belgium in 1999, the 56th anniversary of his landing in the apple tree. He found the spot but the apple tree, alas, was gone.

Sam Jones House

SAM JONES, WHAT ARE YOU DOING HERE?

A Farce
Based on Actual Events

SET:

Looking into living area of the Jones home. On the right is Sam Jones's bedroom which contains a large Victorian bed with the headboard toward the right wall, windows on either side of the bed which are the old style that go all the way to the floor. On the far side of the bed is a table and lamp, other usual furniture is included. There is a doorway from the bedroom into the living room that is the center of the set, which contains a couch, rocking chair and other chairs, table and other Victorian style furniture. There is a stairway at the rear wall going up with a door at the top of the stairs. Another doorway is to the left of the rear wall of the living room, which leads to an apartment. On the left wall of the living room is a doorway to outside. There is a table with a telephone near that door.

CHARACTERS:

SAM JONES	38 year old bachelor
ELLA MAY JONES	40-year-old unmarried sister, legal secretary for her brother, Robert Lee
RUTH JONES	45 year old unmarried sister, a school teacher
RAY & YVONNE CHEAIRS	A middle aged couple who rent an apartment in the Jones house. Mr. Cheairs is the manager of an ice cream factory.
BUDDY MORTON	35 year old acquaintance who enjoys an imbibing good time
MR. A.T. MORTON	Father of Buddy

Robert E. Jones

A.C. ARRINGTON   Hunting friend of Buddy
MICKEY   German Shepard pet and watch dog of the Jones'

SETTING:

About a week before Christmas in the Jones home, a Victorian two story residence in a small town in Mississippi.

SCENE I: About 10:00 P.M. on a Saturday night about a week before Christmas. Sam, Ella May and Ruth are seated in the living room with Mickey. Ruth and Sam are reading. Ella May is shelling pecans.

ELLA MAY: **Sam, I'm so glad you're back home. I feel so much safer now with you <u>and</u> Mickey here.**

RUTH: **Yes, I do too.**

SAM: **Aw, there's no reason to be afraid here, with or without me as long you have Mickey. Boy, you'll know whenever anyone is prowling around immediately. You can watch him and see him perk up his ears and become alert when somebody just walks past the house and, just like me, he's a very light sleeper, will wake up at the slightest noise.**

RUTH: **Yes and if anyone puts one foot in our yard, he knows it and will let us know it for sure, Mmph! He can bark so loudly.**

ELLA MAY: Yes, I know it. Sometimes it's disturbing but it's worth it. You know, all the colored folks know he's here and they always cross to the other side of the street when they get near our house. They don't want any part of him.

RUTH: And you know, Sam, when you drive into the driveway he knows it's you and will jump and whine and scratch on the door to get out, but, boy if any stranger steps in the yard it's completely different. He's ready to tear them up.

RUTH: You remember that time he chased the milkman up in the pecan tree. Boy, he was scared to death. Poor young fellow.

ELLA MAY: That was Ephriam Sellers, wasn't it?

RUTH: That's right, it sure was. He quit the dairy right after that, joined the marines and went overseas.

SAM: Yes, that was right before I was drafted.

ELLA MAY: He married that Wilson girl; Sam Wilson's daughter the week before he left.

RUTH: Then she had an affair with the laundry truck driver. What was his name?

ELLA MAY: Chester Sanders.

RUTH: And she divorced the Sellers boy before he came home for his first leave and people never could tell whether her baby favored the Sellers or the Sanders.

ELLA MAY: **Ruth!**

RUTH: **Then Chester married Lucy Baker and they had about ten children.**

ELLA MAY: **Six.**

RUTH: **Lucy worked for the paper, Mr. Harrison's paper, THE ADVERTISER.**

ELLA MAY: **No, Ruth it was the WEEKLY Leader, because I remember, before she started going with Chester, Robert Watson, delivered the paper—you remember his mother. Lucy Tanner married John Watson when he was sixty-nine years old and she was only thirty-four. They had the one son Robert.**

RUTH: **I thought Robert was Taylor Watson's boy.**

ELLA MAY: **No. Ruth, Taylor Watson moved away from here before Robert was born.**

RUTH: **Didn't he just disappear? Nobody ever heard from him.**

ELLA MAY: **Well, they said at the mill that over $3000 was missing but they couldn't prove anything. It nearly killed his mother, Amanda Seale Watson. She was Judge Seale's daughter, you know.**

RUTH: **Well, I, I believe I'll go on to bed and finish studying my Sunday school lesson in bed. Come on, Mickey, you come on upstairs with me.**

ELLA MAY: **I'm going to finish shelling these pecans and I'll be up. I've got to finish them for the fudge for the Christmas boxes.**

RUTH: **Ella May, why did you peel that bowl of grapes in the kitchen?**

ELLA MAY: **I didn't peel them. I thought you did.**

RUTH: **No, I didn't peel them.**

(Both look at Sam, who is still reading the paper.)

ELLA MAY: **Sam, did you peel those grapes in the kitchen?**

SAM: **What?**

ELLA MAY: **Did you peel those grapes in the kitchen?**

SAM: **Oh, yeah, Mickey loves grapes, you know, but he won't eat them unless they're peeled. So I always peel some for him.**

(Sam returns to reading the paper while Ruth and Ella May stare at him in wonderment.)

SAM: **What?**

RUTH: **Goodnight.**

SAM: **Goodnight, Ruth.**

RUTH: **Goodnight, Sugar.**

(Ruth and Mickey exit upstairs.

SAM: Ella May, I sure am glad to be back home again. It's just so peaceful and serene and...so restful. I've had enough stress and turmoil and...confusion in the Army to last me a lifetime.

ELLA MAY: Sam aren't you proud of how Brother Miller is preaching on the evils of alcohol? I'm so glad we have a courageous minister like him. I don't see how anybody could drink that horrible stuff with all the grief it causes. Don't they know it's <u>against</u> <u>the</u> <u>law</u>!

SAM: (Barely glancing up from newspaper) **Uh-huh.**

ELLA MAY: **I'm so thankful you don't drink. I'm so glad none of my brothers drink.**

SAM: (glances up and stares briefly at Ella May—an almost imperceptible shake of head).

ELLA MAY: **Neither did Papa or Grandpaw. But you know about our cousin Aubrey! He apparently inherited it from grandma's side of the family. So it may be in our blood, so you must be careful!**

SAM: **Ella May, you know I was in the army air corps for three years and, you know, sometimes we'd take a little drink or a beer...**

ELLA MAY: **Oh Sam I know, I understand. I know soldiers facing possible death from a vicious enemy, you know, I can excuse that. Don't feel guilty over it. Those were dreadful frightful days.**

SAM: Ella May, I never got out of Florida.

ELLA MAY: Oh, but you could have been sent overseas in a moments notice! It's all right, I understand.

SAM: (Sigh)

ELLA MAY: It's about time for Ray and Yvonne to get home from the picture show, isn't it?

SAM: Yes, the movie should be over by now.

ELLA MAY: Sam I wish you could find a wife like Yvonne. She's such a nice girl...

SAM: I will some day. Don't worry.

ELLA MAY: Well, I just hate to see a wonderful Christian man like you not married, when there's so many nice deserving girls out there.

SAM: Yes, well...

ELLA MAY: Have you met that new girl at the bank? She's the daughter of John David Sullivan from down at Sweet Springs out west of Green Valley Church, you know.

You know, Mr. Sullivan was married to Mary Joyce Thompson, Jim Thompson's daughter, for about ten years and she up and left him. Robert Lee got him a divorce in 1926 and then he married Jane Ellen Crawford, Thomas Ed Crawford's daughter. They had just this one child, a pretty little thing, cute as a button, and smart! You remember Jane Ellen Crawford don't you, went to our church for a while then changed to Presbyterian 'cause she didn't like Brother Johnson, said he was too liberal, didn't even believe in Adam and Eve. Anyway, this girl's name is Cynthia Louise, I think.

VOICE FROM UPSTAIRS: **Cynthia Lucille!**

ELLA MAY: **That's right, Cynthia Lucille. She joined the, uh, Sam, are you listening?**

SAM (who appears to have dozed a bit): **Oh yes, Ella May, I was just resting my eyes a bit, but I believe I'll go to bed now. I'm a little beat from picking up all those pecans this afternoon.**

ELLA MAY: **Well, you did work hard. Why don't you go on to bed?**

SAM: **I believe I will. Goodnight.**

ELLA MAY: **Goodnight, Honey.**

(A sound at the back door).

ELLA MAY: **Oh, I guess that's Ray and Yvonne.**

SAM: **Well, I'm going on to bed. They will want to tell the whole story of the movie and I would like to see it before it leaves here.**

(Sam exits to bedroom.)

(Enters Ray and Yvonne, taking off topcoats.)

RAY: **Hi, Ella May.**

YVONNE: **Hello, Ella May, everybody gone to bed?**

ELLA MAY: **Yes, they just…**

YVONNE: **You should see that movie! It's wonderful! It's all about this Royal Canadian Mountie, Nelson Eddy, who's tracking down this gang of murderers and when he finds them, they capture him! But this girl, Jeanette McDonald, is their cook or something and they fall in love. They sing to each other so beautifully, "Ah, sweet mystery of life", and then you won't believe this, just as they are about to kill Nelson Eddy…**

(Sam, in his bedroom, covers his ears with pillow.)

RAY: **Yvonne, don't tell her the story. She might want to see it.**

(Sam, relieved, takes pillows from ears.)

YVONNE: **Do you plan to see it, Ella May?**

ELLA MAY: **No, no what happened?**

(Sam jams pillows over ears and turns up the radio, loudly.)

YVONNE: (startled by the noise of the radio): **Goodness! What's going on in Sam's room?**

ELLA MAY: **I guess he's trying to get the news. Sam, would you turn down the radio please?**

(Sam grudgingly turns off the radio.)

YVONNE: **Oh well, it's late. I'll tell you all about it in the morning. Goodnight. Oh, by the way, they certainly are having a big party over at Miss Laura's house. Cars parked all up and down, almost down to our house.**

ELLA MAY: **Yes, I know. It's some of those Yankees who came here with the garment plant. I hear they serve cocktails—the liquor just flows like a fountain.**

YVONNE: **Really?**

RAY: **Come on, Yvonne, let's go to bed. Goodnight Ella May.**

(Ray and Yvonne exit the door to the left.)

ELLA MAY: (as they are leaving): **Goodnight. Nearly 11:00. I'd better get to bed.**

(Turn out lights and goes upstairs.)

SCENE II: A few hours later. Sam is snoring loudly in his bed. Clock strikes 3:00. Buddy Morton dressed in sport coat and tie, disarrayed, wearing a sporty hat, clumsily opens window in Sam's bedroom. The window is the type that goes all the way to the floor. Buddy, humming "Sweet Adeline" enters, walking right into the bedside table knocking the lamp over, ignores it, groping his way around the bed and after much fumbling and stumbling takes off tie neatly folding it up and then draping it over foot of bed, takes off shoes, dropping each one noisily. Meanwhile, Sam is sleeping soundly and snoring throughout all of the commotion. Buddy then proceeds to try to set alarm clock, grumbles at the clock, finally gets in bed, still fully clothed, including hat, and pulls up covers to eye level and lets out a long, deep sigh. At the sound of the sigh. Sam's snoring suddenly ceases and he is awake, motionless, and not breathing. He slowly, slowly rises up in bed, peers around in the semi-darkness, sees nothing, but knows instinctively that someone is there. Reaches over to turn on the lamp, can't find the lamp, realizing for sure something is amiss.

SAM: **Who's there?** (Softly)

(No answer.)

SAM: **Who is there?** (Forcefully but fearfully)

VOICE FROM BED: **'s 'me!**

SAM: (Shocked) **What the _____!** (Jumps backwards out of bed, finds lamp turns it on, puts on table. Looks at figure in bed, overcomes fear, now motivated by anger.)

SAM: **Who do you think you are!** (Grabs cover and jerks it down to expose Buddy Morton in all his splendor, crouched in the bed in the fetal position.)

BUDDY: **Put that damn cover back up! It's cold as hell in here!** (Sam reacts to the commanding voice and dutifully replaces the cover muttering an apology. Suddenly, anger regains control, and he pulls the cover back down again enough to see who the intruder is.)

SAM: **Why, Buddy Morton, what in the world are you doing in my bed?**

BUDDY: **Trying to get some damn schlep! Now turn out the light and leave me alone!**

(His speech is slurred, typical of intoxicated person.)

SAM: **Well, I never**—(Turns out lamp and starts out, stops, turns back toward bed, holds up a pointing finger and starts to speak, but finally exasperated, stomps out of bedroom into living room. Ella May is descending the stairs in robe with curlers, cold cream on her face, etc.)

ELLA MAY: **Sam**, (in a loud whisper) **Sam, what is it?**

SAM: **Ella May, you won't believe it.**

ELLA MAY: **What? What?**

SAM: **Buddy Morton is in my bed.**

ELLA MAY: **Buddy Morton in your bed! Sam, you must have had a nightmare.**

SAM: **I'm not having a nightmare. Buddy Morton is in my bed. Come and see.**

(Ella May tentatively creeps to bedroom door, peeps in and sure enough, there is Buddy Morton, wheezing and snorting in the bed. Ella May tiptoes back out of bedroom.)

ELLA MAY: **Well, what is Buddy Morton doing in your bed?**

SAM: **Ella May, I don't know what he's doing in my bed. I guess he's sleeping.**

ELLA MAY: **How in the world did he get in?**

SAM: **He pulled that big window open next to my bed.**

ELLA MAY: **Oh, that's good.**

SAM: **Good!?**

ELLA MAY: **Well, Ruth and I haven't been able to get that window open for over thirty years.**

ELLA MAY: **Well, what are we going to do about it?**

SAM: **I don't know.**

ELLA MAY: **Should we call the police?**

SAM: **No, he's just drunk. No, don't call the police.**

ELLA MAY: **Drunk! Let me see**. (Having never observed a drunk at close range, she puts on her glasses and tiptoes back into bedroom, peers closely down at the reposing curiosity. Buddy lets out a snort or belch, startling Ella May, who beats a hasty retreat back to the safety of the living room.)

I knew it! What did I tell you about those Yankees! Cocktails!...You're right though; I don't think we should call the police. What would the neighbors think? Oh! and publicity! Oh no, we might have to go to court. They might even think we were accomplices!

SAM: **Oh, Ella May, don't be ridiculous. Maybe we should call an ambulance.**

ELLA MAY: **Good heavens, with a siren!**

SAM: **Well, maybe they could drive without turning it on.**

ELLA MAY: **What would we tell them to do with him and who would pay for the ambulance? They charge $10 you know. You remember that time when that man passed out on our front walk and Ruth thought he was dying and called the ambulance and it turned out to be only a drunk? And after that, Ruth would walk two blocks out of the way so as not to pass in front of Hartman's Funeral Home because she was afraid they would want her to pay the $10.**

SAM: **Okay, never mind.**

Mississippi Gumbo

ELLA MAY: I know! You know at one time Buddy had a heart attack. Dr. Jack is his doctor. He'll know what to do. Let's call Dr. Jack.

SAM: Well, I guess so. He's so sensible. Since Buddy has had a heart attack, that's not a bad idea.

ELLA MAY: Yes, I'll feel much better with Dr. Jack advising us.

SAM: (Goes to telephone) What's his number?

ELLA MAY: 272 I think. No, that's the Jitney Jungle. Uhh, 198, I remember now, it's one more number that Robert Lee's office number which is 197.

SAM: (to telephone) Operator, 198 please. Yes, Operator, that's Dr. Jack's number.

No. no trouble. 198 please. (Delay) I hate to wake him up...Oh, hello Dr. Jack, Sam Jones here. Uh, Jack...no, Ruth and Ella May are fine, there's no problem, but well, yes there is a problem. (Pause) Well, Buddy Morton is in my bed. (Pause)

Well, I don't know what he is doing in my bed. He's just sleeping I think. (A little irritated). He came in through the porch window during the night and got in bed with me. I don't know when. I woke up and, Dr. jack, Dr. Jack! I know it sounds funny to you but it's not funny to us. After all, he's had a heart attack and what if he were to have another. He's too drunk to wake up. Well, we wanted to know what we ought to do...Sleep it off? For how long? We've got to go to Sunday school and church in the morning. We've got company coming for dinner...

Well, all right. Thank you. Sorry to have disturbed you. Goodnight, uh, uh, morning, good morning. Yes, we'll see you at church.

ELLA MAY: What did he say?

SAM: Says just let him sleep it off.

ELLA MAY: SLEEP IT OFF!

SAM: Yes, sleep it off.

ELLA MAY: Well, how long does it usually take? Tomorrow's Sunday, you know.

SAM: Yes, today's Sunday, you mean.

ELLA MAY: We've got Sunday school and church and company coming for dinner.

SAM: I know all that! Didn't you hear me tell him?

ELLA MAY: Oh, merciful heavens, what can we do?! (Wringing hands) We can't leave him there in the bed with the Walls and Brother Taylor coming for dinner after church. What if he staggered out drunk and half dressed while they were here?

Oh Lord, what can we do?! Maybe we can just not go to church. Tell people Ruth's got a cold or something; cancel the dinner.

SAM: What about Dr. Jack? He'll probably tell everyone at church anyway.

Mississippi Gumbo

ELLA MAY: Oh no! But doctors are not supposed to tell confidential matters about their patients. He wouldn't tell anybody, would he? Oh my goodness!

SAM: He'll probably only tell his wife, his closest friends and his Sunday school class.

ELLA MAY: Oh, no, we shouldn't have called him.

SAM: We've got to get him out of here. We've got to call his father and tell him to come get him.

ELLA MAY: Yes! You're right. His father must come get him.

SAM: I'll look up the number. Where's the phone book?

ELLA MAY: Under the sack of pecans.

(Sam gets book looks up number while Ella May wrings her hands.)

ELLA MAY: Why didn't Mickey bark?

SAM: I don't know. Oh, if Mrs. Moreton answers I'll just disguise my voice.

Operator, 374J please. Yes operator, everything is all right. Yes, that's Mr. Morton's number. Uh, uh, don't worry, just ring it please...Oh, operator, is that you Sara, I didn't recognize your voice. Well, I can't explain it all now, but Buddy is in my bed and we can't get him out, and (loudly) I don't know what he's doing in my bed! Just ring the number, please. Thank you. No, that's all right. Yes, I know.

It's lonely there at night. (Pause) **Hello. Hello.** (Speaking in tight strained voice with foreign accent) **Ah, Mizzes Mor-ton, could I pleeze speek with Meester Mor-ton?**

(Pause) **Uh, why yes,** (Aside) **She recognized my voice.** (Resumes normal voice)

Yes, this is Sam Jones. No everything is fine, she's fine, she's fine too. Yes, it is a little early, a beautiful morning isn't it? Thank you, I'll wait. (Whispers to Ella May) **Sounds like a party going on over there...Oh, hello Mr. Morton, Sam Jones.**

Mr. Morton, (pause) **no thank you, but I...I don't think I can come over. No, I don't drink much now; I've got to be getting ready for Sunday school soon.**

Thank you though, I appreciate it. Well, goodbye to you too. No, wait! Mr. Morton, Buddy is over here in my bed. I said, "In my bed." Yes, Buddy, your Buddy. Well I don't exactly know what he's doing in my bed except sleeping, **but you've...Well, he climbed in the window, climbed—in—the—window. If you could get them to stop the music for a minute. Hello, Mr. Morton, Mr. Morton, well I didn't think you would think it's so funny.**

	Hunting! Well, it's about 4:00 now, I think. We'll expect you right over. No thank you, I don't go hunting on Sunday. (Hangs up telephone.)
ELLA MAY:	What did he say?
SAM:	He wanted to know what he was doing in my bed! He sounded drunker than Buddy, but he said he and A.C. and Buddy were supposed to go duck hunting this morning and it's about time for them to go and they'll be right over to get him.
ELLA MAY:	He's in no condition to go hunting.
SAM:	You want to let him just sleep it off?
ELLA MAY:	Oh, no, no, uh, I guess the fresh air will do him good.
SAM:	Do you realize that in all this commotion neither Mickey nor Ruth have uttered a peep? I'll bet they have just slept through the whole thing.
ELLA MAY:	A robber could have just cut off your head, as far as they're concerned.
SAM:	Let's go up and see about them.
ELLA MAY:	Yes.

(Exit up stairs.)

(Yvonne comes out of apartment door, very sleepily, looks around, walks to Sam's door, looks in, sees sleeping figure, quietly closes bedroom door, returns to apartment.)

YVONNE: (As she re-enters apartment) **Ray, I know I heard something.**

RAY: **Aw, Hell, you're always hearing things. If it'd been something. Mickey'd be barking up a storm.**

(Car horn sounds outside.)

LOUD VOICES FROM OUTSIDE BACK DOOR: **Buddy, Buddy,** (someone singing)

Nights are long since you went away, my buddy, my buddy, (Laughter) (knock, knock, knock) **Buddy, Buddy, Sam, Sam.** (Sounds of duck calls—**"Quack, quack, QUACK!"**)

(Door of apartment opens again and Yvonne in curlers, cold cream and robe peeks out, nervously goes to back door.)

YVONNE: **Yes?**

MR. MORTON: **Oh, hi, Yvonne. Sam called us to come over. Is he here?**

YVONNE: **Well, yes, he's asleep. Won't you come in? I'll go get him, if you like?**

MR. MORTON: **Yeah, tell him that "Meester Morton" is here.**
(Nudges A.C. as they exchange smirks.)

(She walks to Sam's door glancing back. Mr. Morton and A.C. who have entered are dressed in duck hunting clothes, smiling broadly and weaving slightly. Yvonne enters Sam's room after getting no response to gentle knocks on the bedroom door. She raps gently on the inside of door, calling softly and sweetly.)

YVONNE: **Sam, Sam, two gentlemen are here to see you.**

(She walks over and gently shakes the shoulder of the sleeping figure.)

BUDDY: (without raising up in the bed): (Loud Voice) **What in the damn hell do you think you're doing in my room? Leave me alone, get out of here and don't let the damn doorknob hit you in the ass as you go out. Who do you think I think you are anyway?**

(Yvonne in speechless shock, aghast to the extreme, backs out, backs down the hall, clutching her mouth, then turns sobbingly and runs into the apartment. A.C. and Mr. Morton watches her, perplexed.)

A.C.: **Well, that sounds like Buddy in there all right.**
MR. MORTON: **Yeah, let's go get him up. We got to get going.**
(They go into Sam's room. A.C. and Mr. Morton work on getting Buddy up, trying to arouse him without much success. At this time Ruth, Ella May and Sam

come walking down the stairs with Sam leading the way.)

SAM: Yes, Ruth. (Disgustedly) **I said Buddy Morton is in my bed drunk.**

RUTH: **Well, what's he doing in your bed?**

ELLA MAY: **Ruth, what a dumb thing to say! He's just there. He's drunk!**

SAM: **What's he doing in your bed! WHAT'S HE DOING IN YOUR BED!! Can't anybody say anything except WHAT'S HE DOING IN YOUR BED?!!!!**

(Apartment door opens just as Sam reaches the bottom step. Out comes irate Ray. Yvonne is seen huddling behind him.)

RAY (confronting Sam, nose to nose): **SAM JONES, WHAT IN THE WORLD DO YOU MEAN TALKING TO MY WIFE LIKE THAT?!**

RUTH (looking around Sam): (Sweetly) **Good morning, Ray.**

SAM: **Ray!**

RAY: **You have no right to shout and curse at her and then insult her!**

SAM: **Ray!**

ELLA MAY: (Sweetly) **Good morning, Ray.**

RAY: **You must think we are damn fools to take something like this. We are moving out first thing** in the morning. And I have half a mind to whip your...

SAM: Ray, Ray, wait a minute! I haven't even seen Yvonne this morning. She must have had a nightmare.

RAY: Nightmare, Hell! She went in your room to wake you up and...

SAM: Oh! That was Buddy. Don't mind him.

RAY: Buddy! What are you talking about?

SAM: Buddy Morton. He's in my bed.

RAY: What?

SAM: Yeah, come and see.

(All walk to Sam's room. Sam opens the door. Ray looks in.)

RAY: Well, I'll be damned. What in the hell is he doing in your bed?!

(Sam restraining himself, patiently looks skyward. Mr. Morton and A.C. are still working on Buddy. Finally, they raise him erect.)

BUDDY: Morning dad! Hi, A.C.

(He is dragged in vertical position past Sam. He is puzzled at the presence of Sam Jones.)

BUDDY: **Sam Jones! What in the Hell are you doing here?**

SAM: **I live here! This is my house! That is my bed!**

What were you doing in my bed!

BUDDY: **I'm sorry. I'm sorry.**

SAM: **Aren't you all going to be late for your hunt? It will soon be light.**

MR. MORTON: **Right, yeah let's go men, let's go.**

(The three musketeers boisterously march out, Buddy's feet dragging.)

SAM: **Have a nice hunt.**

As the trio exits, RUTH calls out a neighborly goodbye: **Ya'll come back any time!**

ELLA MAY: (Flabbergasted) **Ruth!**

RAY: (To Sam) **I'm sorry, Sam. I had no idea.**

YVONNE (who has crept up from the rear): **Sam, what in the world was he doing in your bed?** (Sam's eyes glaze over.)

RUTH: **Yvonne, don't be dumb, he was just there—sleeping!**

ELLA MAY: **Well, in all my born days I've never been through anything like this.**

RUTH: **How did he get in? When did he get in? Do you think he was really drunk?**

ELLA MAY: **Ruth, off all the dumb things, of course, he was drunk.** (Now an authority) **Drunker than anyone I've ever seen. What did I tell you about those Yankees' parties? I told you they would serve cocktails.**

RUTH: **Was that A.C. Arrington with Mr. Morton? Wasn't his mother Janie Brownlee, Mr. Sam Brownlee's daughter from Wesson? Her grandfather was manager of the mill at Wesson.**

ELLA MAY: **Yes, Ruth.**

RUTH: (Continues) **They lived next to Dr. Rowan's house, didn't they? He got killed walking down the railroad tracks one Thanksgiving, when the train came up from behind, blew its whistle and he never looked around. Changed from one track to another, thought the train was on the northbound track but it turned out it was a switcher on the southbound track, and busted into him and knocked him a hundred feet. Killed him deader than a dried worm.**

(Ray and Yvonne throw up hands and return to apartment.)

ELLA MAY: **He left three daughters. One of them married Tom McIntyre's oldest son, Jeff, you know. He became a surgeon and one of the best in the South.**

RUTH: I thought he was a banker. You know, the one that got caught stealing money.

ELLA MAY: **No, Ruth. That was Tom's nephew from Hazlehurst, Jim McIntyre, got sent to Parchman and became a Baptist preacher when he got out.**

(Ella May and Ruth start up stairs.)

RUTH: **Wasn't he preaching that revival down at Norfield when you went down there that time with Charles Perkins?**

ELLA MAY: **No, Ruth, that was Brother DeMent from Meridian and I wasn't with Charles Perkins. I went with William Henry. You remember.**

RUTH: **Goodness gracious!** (Turns at top of stairs.) **Sam, she never forgets anything. Has the memory of an elephant.**

ELLA MAY: **Well, look who's here.**

(Mickey appears on stairs, wagging tail.)

SAM: **Yes, Mickey, I know what you're saying, "What in the Hell was he doing in your bed?"**

(Ruth and Ella May continuing typical conversation as before, fade out after entering door at the top of stairs. Sam, left alone, stands

Mississippi Gumbo

center stage listening to the last sounds of his sister's conversation, silent, facing audience, a la Jack Benny, as the curtain closes.)

Robert E. Jones

Edgewood

THE HOMECOMING

The constant clickity clack of the bumpy train nearly hypnotized Elizabeth as she peered morosely from the hot dank atmosphere of the day coach at the passing scenery of the chalky hillsides of western Alabama approaching the Mississippi line. She thought, "Only about four more hours and I'll be home. I wonder how Robert Lee will feel. I hate to face Daddy, and that wife of his—oh I don't care what she says or what she thinks—I'm over 21 and she can't say or do anything to hurt me now."

Her Virginia classmates had laughed when she told them her beau's given name was "Robert Lee".

"Why do so many of you Mississippians have double names? But, if it's Robert E. Lee, that's okay with us!"

"Oh, if only"—her thoughts traced back to when she was sent off to school in Virginia by her stepmother Vivienne. "Why had Daddy let her make me go?" She had tried to convince Robert Lee that they could go ahead and get married but he, so damn sensible as always, had argued that he couldn't until he had become admitted to the bar so he could make them a living. "I'm only a traveling court reporter- trying to learn law—and can't even make enough to support myself," he had said.

Oh, how she had fumed, argued, and finally given up in disgust. Didn't he have any adventure or romance in his soul? One has to take life when one can get it! Doesn't one?

She dreamily thought back further—to her own mother, her own sweet, beautiful, talented, joyful, tender mother. Oh, if only she hadn't died so young, at 32. But she had, and Father had changed from a fun-loving, adventurous, happy man to an introverted, restrained, listless and distant shell which failed to improve after his rebound remarriage to the calculating and ambitious young Vivienne.

The number two wife quickly had a child of her own—to seal the bargain? - And then lost interest in domestic matters, eagerly trying to scale the social mountain of the small Southern community in a grand manner and to enjoy to the hilt the wealth of her lumber baron husband—encouraging the sale of the lumber business and the move to the larger and more sophisticated town of Brookhaven from the little lumber village of Norfield. And then the building of her dream house—the grandest, finest mansion in town—inlaid mahogany floors, leather walled library, curly pine wainscoting, marble statutes from Italy, crystal chandeliers from England and the grand stairway with Winged Victory at the top, greeting visitors. Oh, it had to be the finest—and it was. If there was one thing for which Elizabeth could thank Vivienne, it was for building Edgewood, the beautiful white columned house on the hill. Elizabeth loved that home. In spite of all, she had had some happy times there in her high school days. Playing tennis in the side yard, roaming the adjoining woods, picking muscadines, swimming in the creek and the simple

Mississippi Gumbo

gatherings on the great front porch of the house. Teasing boys, hiding behind the columns, and taking photographs with her box Kodak.

But why did she have to be so cruel—downright mean. And why did Father allow her to do it?

She remembered that second Christmas in 1916 after being sent off to school in Virginia. Vivienne had written and told her and sister, Fannie, that they couldn't afford for them to come home for the holidays and she was sorry but they would have to stay at school until summer. Elizabeth knew she was actually planning a big party and didn't want Elizabeth and her friends milling about the house.

Resisting Fannie's pleadings, Elizabeth had taken the diamond ring left to her by her mother and pawned it for train fare home, telegraphed that she was coming and caught the first train home. But, oh! What a greeting! She remembered being met by her father and Vivienne, not allowed to get off the train, and ordered to ride on to New Orleans and then return by the next train to Virginia.

It was no wonder that train rides brought a nostalgic ache to her. She remembered when as a six year old she took the slow thirty-mile funeral train ride from Norfield to Hazlehurst, when her beloved mother's body was transported for burial. The engineer had known her mother and no one had ever heard such mournful calls of a steam whistle as was sounded at every crossing. It seemed that even the locomotive itself grieved for the sweet departed May. For many years thereafter every distant train whistle was painful for her.

Elizabeth remembered that upon return to Virginia, the country had entered the war and the girls at school were knitting socks and sweaters for the boys overseas. Elizabeth mischievously put her name and address in a sock and to her delight, a month later, received a letter from a doughboy in France.

The exchange of letters was avidly followed by the other girls in the school as a romance began to blossom. The excitement of the eager friends reached an ecstatic peak when the soldier Romeo wrote that he was coming home and would rush to visit Elizabeth as soon as he arrived.

Predictably, the romance bore fruit, encouraged by the jubilant schoolmates and helped by the sense of rejection, bitterness and loneliness in Elizabeth resulting from the treatment by her stepmother and the refusal of her longtime sweetheart to wed.

She had married the boy—suddenly—announcing it afterwards in a curt telegram to her father and stepmother.

It wasn't long afterwards that she realized with dread and a sinking feeling that the marriage couldn't last. He was uneducated, taciturn and a heavy drinker, although he was often kind and tender to her, they never seemed to be able to get on the same level intellectually or emotionally, and stayed worlds apart. The early romantic excitement had faded and died. She had been determined to endure the marriage because of what her stepmother would say, but eventually she knew it was hopeless. The hell of continuing the farce was too big a price to pay for her pride. She left—now pregnant- to live with her sister in Savannah. She filed for and obtained a divorce in Georgia. The baby was stillborn after an agonizingly prolonged labor.

And now, finally, she was coming home. It was not to be a joyous homecoming, but at least this time she was assured she would be able to get off the train. She had wired Robert Lee to meet her and he had wired back joyously that he would and that he loved her. The thought of his steadfast love through all that had transpired brought haunting tears to her eyes. If he could still love her and if he were still willing to marry her, she would make him the best, the most loving and faithful wife a man ever had!

She knew too that Father would be there. She had wired him too and he had replied simply that he would meet her.

As the train pulled into the familiar station, she could see from the depot lights a steady drizzle slowly drifting downward. It was as though someone had chosen the most appropriate weather for her homecoming. She could see Robert Lee standing alone, hatless, and peering through the blackness searching for a glimpse of her. And there was her father, properly attired in raincoat, hat and umbrella, with faithful servant, Will, eagerly waiting nearby to carry her bags.

She refused to allow herself the physical luxury of tears as she descended the steps to the platform and received the joyful but restrained welcome of Robert Lee. They embraced silently—a few words now would be meaningless. Her father looked older and sadder as he too greeted her with a silent embrace.

Only Will, gathering the bags, could muster a verbal greeting, "It sho is nice to have you home, Miss Liz," as the four slowly walked in the rain to the waiting car.

TRIMBLE'S BARBERSHOP

Back in 1972, I got an inspiration to write a feature story about Trimble's Barber Shop, then located behind Brookhaven Bank just before the alley. It was to be submitted to the Times Picayune Sunday supplement "Dixie."

After interviews with the willing subjects, I dragged Don Jackson to the joint for pictures. It had to have pictures!

The piece was painstakingly written and readied for publication, that is, as soon as the photos were ready. Days and then weeks went by with my repeatedly calling Don for the pix, but always getting very good reasons why they weren't yet ready.

My inquiries slowed to about once every two months, until finally lovable Don confessed he couldn't find them. I gave up.

Then about seven years later, he called to say they had surfaced. Great! But in the meantime some of the subjects had moved on to that great tonsolarium in the sky, so I just filed it all away in my own filing system, which was somewhat similar to Don's. The story and prints remained safely in seclusion somewhere in my office until; suddenly they bobbed to the top again in the '90s. So, here's the story with pictures.

Robert E. Jones

Trimble's-The Steady Hands of Experience

If you don't trust these young whippersnapper hair stylists and demand a little stability and experience for your personal barber, you could hardly do better than visit to Trimble's Barber Shop in Brookhaven where you can draw an accumulated store of 200 years of experience.

The Trimble boys, Maurice and his kid brother, Burton have been barbering together since 1923. The elder Trimble started in 1918 and welcomed his little brother into the tonsorial art five years later. But they are somewhat Johnny-come-latelies compared to the associate, Ham Case, who has been wielding a cutlass since 1912.

The three combined their mowing operations back in 1923 as young blades and now, nearly 50 years later, are still at it—although there have been periods of separation in between. Mr. Case operates the third chair in the present establishment as the dean of Brookhaven barbers, shown in the photo on his 85th birthday. So, Mr. Case carries 60 years experience followed by Maurice with 54 and Burton with 49.

Throw in the 37 years of continuous shoe-shining activities of "Red," also known as Sylvester Robinson, and you have two solid centuries of know-how in the one shop.

"Red" has helped five children through college by beautifying Brookhaven's feet. His three sons have assisted him from time to time, but no one has ever out shined "Red."

The leather field seems to naturally bring out the best in "Red." Not only does he have a feather touch in coaxing beauty from shoes, but also he has exhibited quite a talent for prognosticating pigskin performances in the fall. Many local football experts get their "inside" tips straight from Red.

ANCIENT WALL ADS

Adorning the wall opposite the barber chairs are some ancient mirrors bearing white frosted letter advertisements placed there in 1914. The firms paid a small initial charge when the mirrors were installed and have had the benefit of the displays continuously ever since.

For those few still in business it has been probably one of the greatest bargains in local advertising history. Three of the advertisers are still chugging along, in fact, are very healthy. Brookhaven Bank & Trust Company, C.B. Perkins Hardware and Frank H. Hartman, undertaker, are well known firms.

At the bottom of the latter ad is a photo added a few years later after the installation of the ad, proudly displaying Brookhaven's first ambulance, a shiny new 1926 Cadillac.

Other of the advertisers have been out of business for from 20-40 years, but their sparkling call for customers goes on, such as Crystal Ice Company, "Ice Phone—46; Coal Phone—97"; also L.D. Boadwee, "34 years in same location;" and Hoffman's "That's Where They All Go For Cigars, Stationery and Soda Water, Etc."

Robert E. Jones

77 HOUR WEEK

When the Trimbles and Mr. Case started their clip joint, they worked from seven to seven during the week, sort of pacing themselves and resting up for Saturday, when they went all out from seven in the morning to as soon after midnight as they could take care of all remaining customers. That was a minimum of 77 hours a week. Of course, they took off all day every Christmas and Thanksgiving in addition to Sundays.

Back in those days, Saturday was always a biggie. That was when farmers came to town and got their weekly shave and sometimes a haircut, at the prices of 15 cents and 35 cents.

When Mr. Ham started, most of the shops had one or more bathtubs in the back, and the hardworking farmers dreamed all week of when they could wallow in the luxury of a hot bath followed by a slick barber shave—a ritual lasting up to two hours. An assistant was available to wash their backs and pour in more hot water.

Once a bathing farmer, who had already enjoyed a sip or two of internal pleasures, got his back scalded from a cascade of too hot water from an inexperienced attendant and ran *au naturale* from the shop, proclaiming excitedly that he was being stabbed, with the attendant and three puffing barbers in hot pursuit.

The barbers were finally able to stop the September morn sprint a block later and quickly wrapped their disturbed customer in barber cloth amid the startled gasps of puzzled passersby.

In those early days, it was nearly all shave-shave-shave. In fact, Burton recalls one busy Saturday when he did nothing but shave customers all day long. Nary a haircut. Now he has many busy days with only haircuts.

Also, in those days, every regular customer had his own shaving mug hanging on a rack. Maurice still uses one of these, adorned "John B. Nalty" who was one of Brookhaven's leading citizens of the early part of the century.

Maurice in his early career doubled as beauty operator—in fact, he holds the distinction of performing the town's first "permanent wave," a momentous event in the early '20s. The customer: Mrs. Walter Turnbough. He stills cuts the hair of many ladies of the town.

The Trimble lads and Mr. Ham figure they've done half a million shaves and haircuts so far, give or take a few thousand, and if the crew-cut would only come back in style, they could yet make the million mark. In the meantime, they urge, "If you want to really be trimmed, come to Trimble's."

THE SAUER STORY

He was a most forgiving man. Albert Sauer, a professional photographer, had fallen in love with and married a beautiful Paris, Tennessee, girl, Myrtle Love. She was the daughter of a prominent dentist and owner of a string of racehorses. The couple moved to Brookhaven, Mississippi, to open a photography shop in the early 1920's and established a successful business.

His love and awe for his beautiful wife grew, he often posed her for glamorous pictures, and she maintained a not-so-secret ambition for show business.

As the years passed she longed for excitement and glamorous living, but the earnings of a small town photographer fell far short of her needs. She became a little bored and restless for a better life.

Rumors around town had her involved with a rough 26 year old taxi driver, Ralph Greenlee, who once had been employed to drive Mrs. Sauer and her two little girls to Paris, Tennessee, to visit her folks. Greenlee later became a frequent visitor at the Sauer household, running errands and doing favors for them. Later, in court testimony, it was revealed that he had confided to a close friend that he expected to marry and live with her some day.

The tension building in the triangle reached a climax on the night of Tuesday, December 29, 1931. The Sauers lived in the two story "Montgomery" house at 121 North Second Street. In the backyard was a garage, where they kept their Dodge Coupe, and a studio where he developed his pictures. After supper that evening, Sauer left their kitchen to go out to the studio to do some developing. When he was returning to the house, something heavy hit him in the head, knocking him down, then after a second blow to his head, he lost consciousness.

The scene changes to an area 7 miles northeast of town near the entrance of the "World's Largest Gravel Pit," where the Illinois Central Railroad gravel line passed under the road.

Some black residents of the area on their way home in the early dark of winter, stumbled across Mrs. Sauer lying on the shoulder of the road, moaning, and apparently injured and semi-conscious. They then discovered the wrecked automobile down the embankment and the body of Albert Sauer lying near the car. They hurriedly sought help from the nearby store of Matthew Smith, who rushed to the scene and helped carry Mrs. Sauer to the store and then summoned an ambulance from Frank Hartman's funeral home for the apparently dead, Albert Sauer.

Upon arrival of the ambulance, the medics discovered Sauer was very much alive, but incoherent and semi-conscious.

When questioned, Mrs. Sauer related that she and her husband had gone for a pleasure drive after supper and that he had been driving wildly and she had jumped from the car when it was veering off the road.

Word of the accident spread quickly through the town. Rumors and speculation about the strange event were rampant. In the barbershops and restaurants, there was no other topic of conversation.

A bombshell exploded in the matter when Albert Sauer fully regained consciousness and related to the authorities that he had been viciously assaulted in his back yard and apparently was placed unconscious in the car and driven out to the scene of the "accident."

The local police chief, W. Ed Smith, immediately began an investigation and found a bloody metal bar under the Sauer's backyard studio; blood in the car's trunk; and witnesses who had seen Mrs. Sauer apparently alone, driving their coupe out from their driveway headed towards the gravel pit. Others had seen Mrs. Sauer meeting with Greenlee about an hour before the attack.

The Lincoln County Grand Jury was in session when Chief Smith concluded his investigation and the district attorney, J. W. Cassedy, obtained an indictment January 14th against the lovely wife and the suspected accomplice, Ralph Greenlee, for "assault and battery with a deadly weapon with intent to kill."

The case was hurriedly brought on for trial on Wednesday, January 20, 1932. A jury was impaneled and a two-day trial ensued, conducted by District Attorney, J. W. Cassedy, and aided by Hugh V. Wall, Sauer's personal attorney. The surviving husband was brought in to court, testified from a hospital gurney, and told of the two severe blows to his head and of not regaining consciousness until two days later in the hospital.

Chief Smith testified about finding the bloody steel bar (a spoke from a wagon wheel) hidden under the studio and about the conflicting statements of Mrs. Sauer.

Other witnesses told of having seen Mrs. Sauer driving their car alone, away from their house shortly after the time of the assault.

Other evidence, although all circumstantial, seemed to clearly incriminate the young wife. The presence of her two small daughters in the courtroom was appealing, but insufficient to counter the damning evidence.

A throng of avid citizens as well as reporters attended the trial from Jackson and New Orleans. The old balcony, normally reserved in that era for black spectators, was so jam-packed that Judge Simmons ordered it cleared because it appeared to be at the breaking point.

The jury took the case for deliberation and after over 24 hours of weighing the evidence, came back in to announce they were hopelessly deadlocked, The judge sent them back out, urging them to do their duty and return a verdict. However, after a few more hours, they returned and reiterated that it was hopeless. The frustrated judge declared a mistrial and to the shock of the defendant and her lawyer, Abie Cohn, ordered the case reset for a new trial the <u>NEXT DAY</u>, Friday, January 22nd.

It was reported that the jury had stood at ten votes for conviction and two for acquittal.

The second trial went similarly as the first except Mrs. Sauer testified tearfully, at great length, denying that she had anything to do with it. She claimed that she had also been struck in the head at the house and that she was semi-conscious and vaguely remembered being driven out to the gravel pit. Her story and an impassioned plea by defense attorney, Mr. Cohn, failed to sway the jury and after only a half hour of deliberation, they returned a verdict of "guilty as charged" but recommended the mercy of the court. She was sentenced to serve 3 to 5 years in the state prison. The defendant posted bond and appealed to the Mississippi Supreme Court for a new trial.

END OF STORY?—NOT QUITE

Three days after the conviction of his wife for attempted murder, Albert Sauer, understandably, had his attorney, Hugh V. Wall; file a complaint against her for divorce, alleging adultery and the attempt on his life.

With the conviction for assault with intent to kill, Myrtle Sauer was totally devastated, facing a bleak future. Albert despised Myrtle and was suing for divorce on grounds of adultery and seeking custody of the children, and Myrtle was facing a prison sentence! What was going to happen to her life and to her children? It was then that the old, cagy lawyer, Abie Cohn, earned his fee although he had lost the case.

He told Myrtle to be optimistic; things will work out if she followed his advice. He asked, "Will you do as I say?" Myrtle replied, "Yes, anything."

"All right, your husband is out of the hospital. Invite him home! And TAKE HIM TO YOUR BED!"

She followed this sage advice. Mr. Sauer accepted her kind invitation in all its particulars. A week later, he told his lawyer, Mr. Wall, to drop the divorce case. When he refused, Sauer filed a motion on his own to dismiss the case. Furthermore, he worked night and day to get his wife's conviction overturned. He published a long "exoneration" of his wife in the local papers. It was expressing total faith in her innocence, and timed to appear while the Supreme Court was considering her appeal.

The appeal of the conviction proceeded through the legal channels in all deliberate speed, approaching a decision at the November 1932, session. Shortly thereafter, the Sauer family sold their home and moved to Greenville where they opened a photography shop.

Sauer, in his fervor for his beloved wife, wrote a long detailed, but rambling defense of her and had it published in the Jackson, Mississippi, and Paris, Tennessee papers. He sought to convince readers that his wife had come out of the house just after he had been attacked, surprising the unknown assailants, and that she was struck in the head also, being rendered semi-conscious, and that both she and her husband had been driven out to the gravel pit by the assailants and there dumped with the car.

If the judges read Sauer's public plea, it failed to sway them. They affirmed the conviction.

However, Sauer was undaunted. He circulated petitions addressed to Governor Mike Conner seeking a pardon. He obtained several hundred signors from prominent people in Brookhaven and Greenville.

As required by law a sample petition was published in the local paper November 26, 1932, as follows:

PETITION FOR PARDON

To Governor M. S. Conner, Jackson, Miss.

We, the undersigned citizens for Lincoln County, Mississippi, hereby respectfully request you to grant a pardon to Mrs. Myrtle Love Sauer, because we believe that under all circumstances and conditions existing in her case the same is justified; and, inasmuch as her husband, Mr. A. D. Sauer, the alleged assaulted party, has made a careful investigation of the facts in this case, and has exonerated his wife, and does not believe she is guilty; and inasmuch as their two (2) children are living happily together at this time, we believe that the ends of justice will be promoted by the granting to her of a pardon.

Respectfully,

R. C APPLEWHITE, Sheriff,
DR. G. F. WINFIELD,
JAY McGRATH,
and others.

Many influential people wrote personal letters to the governor urging him to grant the pardon. The governor replied to one of his constituents that the decision he faced in the Sauer case was the most vexing of any pardon request he faced in his term.

From the State Archive records, it is not clear whether the pardon was ever officially granted or whether the governor allowed the matter to drag on and on until his term ended and was eventually ignored. In any event, she never served a day in prison and the loving couple lived happily ever after.

Sheriff Dan Lee

THE OUTLAW, THE SHERIFF AND THE GOVERNOR

None of Joe Loftin's neighbors could conceive of his being the type who would commit such a ghastly crime. He had a pretty wife and two fine children and went to Society Hill Baptist Church every Sunday. His father had been a hardworking, successful farmer of the Oakvale community and had set him up with some good farmland and a house.

It was known that Joe and his older brother, Moses, had been feuding a little—but for him to coolly ambush him at night, shoot him six times, then stab him repeatedly and finally slit his throat was too grisly to contemplate.

The year was 1884, in the Oakvale community of Lawrence County, Mississippi. Joe was 31 years old and had a farm near his mother's place. He and Moses had had several run-ins; the latest was Joe's stealing a bushel of fresh garden peas from Moses. Moses humiliated Joe after he discovered the theft. Accompanied by his two other brothers, he calmly retook the peas from Joe's house, daring Joe to try to stop him.

Joe's resentment of Moses festered and intensified over the following months, and he became obsessed with getting even with his big brother.

Robert E. Jones

One day in August, Joe decided to try to round up his 40 to 50 sheep that he allowed to roam and graze through the countryside, some with bells hanging from their necks. He left home and went by Sandy Martin's cabin where the hard working darky struggled for a living on forty acres, next to Joe's place. Sandy had taken his surname upon emancipation from the "Martin" plantation, which was the source of a national controversy in the Lincoln-Douglas debates in the 1860 presidential campaign after Stephen Douglas' wife had inherited the plantation. Joe asked Marion and Ambrose, Sandy's teenaged son and nephew, to come along with him and help hunt for the sheep. After getting Sandy's permission, they tagged along happily, especially since Joe let Marion, the older, carry Joe's shotgun, loaded with squirrel shot, in case they ran across a rabbit or a squirrel.

Joe was carrying a rifle, and in his vest, the Martin boys had earlier espied a pistol. As they walked down the muddy road on their quest, Joe noticed some fresh horse tracks headed down the road toward Dr. Goss' store. After studying them for some distance, he suddenly mused out loud, "I know whose horse that is!"

The boys asked "Whose?"

"Never mind whose horse it is. I tell you what; you boys go on over there across the woods to that pasture on the other side of the creek. The sheep sometimes lay up there. I'm going on down the road a piece."

The boys didn't like that and said that if they couldn't go with him, they'd just go on home. They then meandered through the woods, still hoping for a squirrel or something to shoot, but generally headed back towards the house.

Shortly thereafter, as they roamed the woods, they heard a shot, then three other louder shots, and some hollering and cursing. They wondered what it was all about but continued slowly on towards home. When they came close to the creek that ran between their place and Joe's, they unexpectedly came upon Joe out in the creek washing his hands and arms and his big knife from what was obviously blood.

They asked Joe what had happened, and how did he get blood all over him. Joe looked up, startled, and angrily told them if they ever told anybody about his washing off blood, he would kill them both.

The frightened boys hurried home.

Earlier that evening Moses Loftin had told his mother that he was going to ride to Dr. Goss's store about two miles up the road. Later at dusk, Moses' horse came trotting up to Mama's house riderless. The two alarmed younger brothers, Crawford and Silas, went searching for him. They rode quickly down the muddy road toward Goss' store and found where Moses' horse had apparently been startled and reared up, and then some ten paces away in the gathering twilight, they found their brother. He was unconscious, moaning and bleeding from multiple wounds, both gun shot wounds and cuts. They hurriedly got him home and sent for Dr. Buford Larkin, but by the time the medical help had arrived, Moses had breathed his last.

Robert E. Jones

There were no eyewitnesses, but the family had little doubt that Moses' death had been the result of the long-standing feud between the two brothers had somehow reached a tragic climax. Crawford and Silas could barely control their fury and wanted to take immediate revenge against their older brother, but the grief stricken mother tearfully persuaded them to let "the Law" handle it. They gave in to their mother and went to the nearby justice of the peace, waking him at midnight, to file charges against Joe for murder.

Early the next morning, the judge deputized two men to arrest Joe and to bring him to the Loftin place for a preliminary hearing. When the arresting officers approached Joe's house Saturday morning, he was sitting on his porch calmly drinking coffee. Joe jovially greeted the officers and invited them to dismount and join him for coffee. They politely refused and told him they had a warrant for his arrest.

"What fer?" says Joe, his face ashen.

"For killing your brother Moses," was the terse reply.

"Is he dead?"

"Yep."

"Did he say anything?"

"Nope," came the reply.

Joe seemed relieved and some color returned to his face, but when the officers said they were taking him to his mother's place for the hearing, he again paled noticeably.

"I ain't welcome there," he pled, but go there he did in the custody of the officers.

Mississippi Gumbo

At the Loftin house were the two principal witnesses, the Martin boys, now almost as pale as the defendant. Taking advantage of a momentary lapse of attention, Joe was able to speak hurriedly and briefly with the two boys. When they testified, they said nothing about the blood cleansing in the creek and even bolstered Joe's case by swearing that in the short time between the gunshots and when they saw Joe at his house afterwards, it would have been impossible for him to have done the shooting.

Since there was no hard evidence to connect Joe with the crime, the judge dismissed the charges and released the relieved but edgy Joe.

On the next day, Sunday, the nearby Society Hill Baptist Church was unusually crowded. As the members gathered, their thoughts were not of Christian serenity. The crowd was abuzz with heated talk of the horrible murder of their friend and neighbor. Most all strongly suspected that their fellow member Joe was the killer.

Among the worshipers were Joe and Lavinia, nervously shy as they mingled with the folks before the services started. Among the comments overheard by Joe and Lavinia were "He's a damned fool if he don't git away from here right away." And "If he's guilty he ought to be hung up afore a trial...the only thing we need for a good lynching is somebody to lead it."

Joe was not oblivious to this vicious chatter and through the sermon began to think that it was probably a darn good time to go visit his friends and kinfolk who a few years before had migrated to Texas.

So, early Monday he packed up and headed for the lone star state for a long visit with friends.

After his departure, interest centered upon the little Martin boys. People visited Sandy Martin more than once with forceful advice as to what the boys should do. There were citizens and neighbors demanding adamantly that they tell the whole truth. Also, there were friends of Joe reminding them not to betray Joe, or they would certainly regret it. It had been bandied about that "If those Martin boys had a rope around their necks, they'd sing a different song."

In a classic case of being "between the rock and a hard place," the Martin boys supported by their terrified father and uncle, Sandy Martin, eventually cracked and told the whole story. From the facts finally related by Marion and Ambrose, and from the other physical evidence gathered at the scene, the truth emerged that Joe had recognized the fresh hoof prints as those of his brother Moses' horse. He had surmised that Moses was going to Goss' store a short distance up the road and would be returning shortly. Hidden in ambush beside the road when the unsuspecting Moses rode by, he shot him at point blank range with his rifle, ran out, fired three pistol shots into him, and then finished him off with stabs and slashes to his head and neck.

As a result, an indictment was obtained against Joe. However, he was in the great state of Texas, and the legal procedure of extradition was complicated and cumbersome and would require the cooperation of the governor of Texas. These hurdles seemed to call for a more imaginative strategy to bring Joe back home.

Mississippi Gumbo

Mrs. Loftin, mourning her first-born and vengeful towards her second, put up a $400 reward of cash gold with the help of her youngest son, Silas, for any law officer who would return Joe to the authorities in Lawrence County. This lure of money bore fruit in an unexpected manner. Someone sent Joe a copy of the reward notice and he got to thinking about it. He took the notice to the local Texas sheriff and offered to surrender and go back with him peacefully to Lawrence County if he would split the reward with him!

The skeptical sheriff telegraphed Lawrence County, got confirmation of the reward, and agreed to the deal. They leisurely rode their way back and checked into the Lawrence County sheriff's office in late January 1885. The reward was duly paid, and the Texas sheriff happily headed back home $200 richer. However, the authorities prudently had Joe confined in the jail at Hazlehurst in the adjoining county, safely away from his cronies and also away from those who would relish seeing him dangle from the highest tree.

A smug Joe, confident of being acquitted, managed to employ two of the top lawyers in south Mississippi, A.C. McNair of Brookhaven and A.H. Longino of Monticello. Undoubtedly his share of the reward came in handy there, however, the Lawrence County deed records indicate that the reward money was woefully inadequate to employ such prominent barristers. A deed dated February 24, 1885, (but not recorded in the public records until after the trial) disclosed the transfer from Joe to lawyer Longino of all of his undivided interest in his father's estate of 720 acres in the Oakvale Community.

Joe was arraigned and pled Not Guilty at the end of the January 1885 term of Lawrence County circuit court, and his trial was set for July in Monticello.

In the interim, while the young star witness Marion Martin was scratching up something to eat for breakfast early one morning around the first of March, someone poked a gun through one of the many cracks of his paw's rickety cabin and blasted him down. About 6 weeks later Marion's cousin Ambrose was plowing a Mr. Armstrong's field, and someone hiding in the edge of the nearby woods gunned him down also. Had these shots proven fatal, the outcome of the Loftin trial would have been problematical. But happily for all but Joe and his cronies, the two hardy black boys survived and recovered sufficiently from their wounds to testify at the July trial. The authorities never found out the identity of the assassins, but Joe himself had a perfect alibi: he was incarcerated and closely guarded in the jail at Hazlehurst, some forty or so miles away.

The populace of the entire county was eagerly awaiting the trial date. Judge A.G. Mayers was to preside over the match between District Attorney G.B. Huddleston, leading the prosecution, and the powerful defense team of fiery A.C. McNair and the golden-tongued A.H. Longino. The young black witnesses were kept at an undisclosed location until the big day.

Figure 1 Crawford Loftin Brother of Joe Loftin

THE TRIAL OF JOE E. LOFTIN

On the trial date, all seats in the courtroom were filled for over an hour before the opening of the proceedings. Without electricity, the only cooling devices were human hands waving hats and fans vainly trying to stir the stuffy air, saturated with the odor of tobacco and sweat, with faint occasional wafts of an alcohol scent. The emotional atmosphere was stifling also, with the heat and the passion of the crowd. Many chronic and avid courtroom watchers had come from surrounding counties but had to wait outside around the courthouse, trying to hear the proceedings through the open windows.

The first witness was the bereaved Mother who bravely but sadly told of the bad blood between the two brothers and of her son Moses being brought to the house on the night of August 24th mortally wounded.

The brother Crawford next testified about how he and Silas, (who had died a few months before the trial) had discovered Moses' horse returning home with an empty saddle and how they had located the moaning and bleeding Moses in the road about a mile from home.

Dr. Buford Larkin described Moses' ghastly and fatal wounds and his death.

Several other witnesses, including the terrified Sandy Martin, testified about various peripheral matters before the crucial star witnesses, Marion and Ambrose Martin, were called to the stand.

The throng packed in the courtroom seemed to hold its breath as they leaned forward as far as possible so as not to miss a word. Mixed in the crowd were members of Joe's gang, undoubtedly including the unsuccessful assassins, glaring at the little witnesses hoping to intimidate them. The rest of the crowd was just as eager to hear what they would say.

District Attorney G.B. Huddleston, his firm and confident voice reverberating through the huge courtroom, questioned young Marion first. Silence engulfed the room as thick as the nauseous air, as the young witness in a soft respectful voice told about the events of the fateful day—about hunting for Joe's sheep; about Joe's recognizing the horse tracks in the road and suddenly sending the boys back; about Joe carrying a rifle; of hearing the shots, and most importantly of having seen Joe washing blood from his knife and his hands and clothes and Joe's furious threat to kill him if he told anyone. Marion confessed to lying to the Justice of the Peace in the preliminary hearing, but only because Joe had threatened to kill him if he didn't. He also testified about having been shot from ambush by an unknown person in March, five months before the trial.

Furious cross examination and finger pointing by Longino could not shake Marion's story. The crowd and the jury seemed to understand and believe that the young witness had been coerced by terror into lying at the preliminary hearing and that his testimony now had the ring of truth.

Longino:	"You believe in God?"
Marion:	"Yas Suh"
Longino:	"You believe in the Bible as God's sacred word?"
Marion:	"Yas"
Longino:	"At the JP, hearing you laid your hand on the Bible and swore to tell the truth, didn't you?"
Marion:	"Yas Suh"
Longino:	"But you LIED to the JP didn't you—you lied, lied, lied! Isn't that right?"
Marion:	"Yas Suh"

Then the famous defense lawyer, feeling he was on a roll, asked one more question:

Longino: "Why did you lie?"

Marion: "Because Mr. Joe done tole me he would kill me if I told what I seed, and I knowed he would too."

A murmur and a rustle emanated from the packed throng and it seemed that the tide had just turned against Joe.

Ambrose followed as the next witness and testified almost identically with Marion's account except he added that earlier on that day he had been in Joe's house and had spotted the stock and trigger of a pistol in the inside pocket of a vest hanging on the wall which Joe later was wearing when they had gone hunting for the sheep.

It is difficult for one to imagine the pressure, and the terror that these youngsters had to undergo. Angry and vicious threats and intimidation from both sides, and there was no Witness Protection Program to protect them. They knew they would have to walk out of the court house after their testimony right through the massive throng of impassioned whites, most of them wanting Joe's head in a noose, but also many armed secret cronies of Joe who would shoot these little black boys down again without a flicker of conscience if they thought they could get away with it.

Their ordeal was a monumental act of courage. They honestly admitted that they had lied to the justice of the peace because they believed that they would be killed if they told the truth. This explanation carried considerable weight when they told of having been shot from ambush before the trial to which testimony the defense attorney vehemently objected.

This was effective to the jury, but unfortunately, allowing the evidence of the attempt on their lives to be presented to the jury proved to be a tactical plunder for the prosecution later.

Many other witnesses testified, including Joe and his wife—denying that the defendant had had anything to do with the killing. The courtroom rafters rattled for hours during the eloquent arguments by the able lawyers while the hand fans furiously fought the Mississippi July heat.

But the evidence of the long-standing feud, prior threats, the opportunity, and most of all the crucial testimony of the two young black neighbors proved convincing beyond a reasonable doubt to the jury and they quickly returned a verdict of guilty, but were unable to agree on the sentence. Under the law at that time, this compelled Judge A.G. Mayers to sentence the defendant "to be hanged by the neck until you are dead." The tension of the community deflated like a balloon expelling its air. However, the relief did not endure.

APPEAL

Longino and McNair prepared an able and full appeal, citing many alleged technical flaws in the proceedings, but the one about letting the jury hear that the chief witnesses had been bushwhacked while Joe was in jail was prejudicial and convinced the Supreme Court that Joe should have a second trial. This cost Joe 80 more acres of land and also his entire interest in the personal estates of his father L.L. Loftin, and of his murdered brother Moses and his recently deceased brother Silas. (Under Mississippi law if he were to be convicted of killing Moses he could not inherit a share of Moses' estate, but if acquitted he would be entitled to a share in all three estates.)

The re-trial was moved to Hazlehurst, and the script went pretty much the same as the first, but without bringing out to the jury the matter of the attempted murder of the witnesses. It was a little easier on the Martin boys this time. They had gotten to be old hands at it and were not quite as intimidated as before.

A guilty verdict came back again, but this time the jury made a recommendation for life imprisonment. This merciful gesture was possibly a tribute to the four-hour closing argument of Mr. Longino. However, Mr. B.T. Hobbs, the Brookhaven editor did not think highly of it, caustically commenting:

> "Many will be surprised to learn that the jury recommended imprisonment for life in the penitentiary as the penalty in this case instead of a hemp halter. If Joe Loftin was guilty at all, he was guilty of one of the foulest crimes in all the calendar, the murder of a brother in cold blood, without a single extenuating circumstance, and should have suffered the full penalty of the law."

So, having escaped the "hemp halter," the relieved lawyers and their client accepted the lifetime sentence and chose to make no further appeals.

Soon Joe bade a sad farewell to his wife and two boys, ages 10 and 5 and boarded the train to the penitentiary in the custody of the sheriff. But his story does not end here.

THE ESCAPE

In those days of 1886, the penitentiary was not large enough to accommodate all the prisoners. Those who were able to work were leased out by the State to perform labor. The state got compensation, the prisoners received "goodtime" on their sentences and the companies leasing the prisoners got cheap labor. At this time nearly all the prisoners were leased to the Gulf and Ship Island Railroad to construct rail lines which ran North and South on the East side of Pearl River- running right through Joe's stomping grounds and on to the coast.

Joe apparently did not take too kindly to the labor of laying cross ties and spiking rails, and within a year of his conviction, he seized a momentary opportunity and made a daring escape from the guards. He tromped through the coastal swamps northward for miles until he reached some high ground, then traveling at night and hiding by day, he finally made his way back to his home territory in South Lawrence County near Oakvale. He was able to elude the authorities for over a year thereafter, sheltered and hidden most of the time by his faithful wife, and at other times lurking in the woods and stealing food where possible.

Numerous thefts and other crimes were attributed to him, during his tenure as a fugitive from August of 1887 to the summer of 1888. Then in late July that year, a young 26-year-old farmer, James Sauls, was "bushwhacked" by unknown parties while he and Joe's young wife Lavinia were rocking on the front porch of one of his tenant farm cabins. The Lawrence County Press reported:

> "Mr. James Sauls, who lives about 10 miles south of this place was shot in the hip and side on last Monday evening while sitting on the gallery of Mrs. Loftin, one of his tenants. Immediately after the shooting, five men were seen running away from their place of concealment, but as yet nothing definite or reliable can be obtained as to who did the shooting, and the whole affair remains a complete mystery. The charge was delivered from a shotgun and at once proved fatal. He lived but a short time, but during that time, he scarcely spoke. It is a very sad affair and is deeply deplored by our citizens who are opposed to bushwhacking."

The perpetrators of this blatant murder were never identified or brought to justice, but the people in the area were convinced it was Joe and his gang.

The outrage of the community rose to a steaming point, and citizens began toting their guns and being on the lookout for Joe, ready to shoot him down on sight. An $800 reward had been posted for him, and frequent sightings of Joe Loftin were the big news at all gatherings in the area.

On August 11th, some of the bounty hunters found him on Mr. A.W.W. Russell's place and quickly opened fire on him. Joe returned the fire but had been hit in the arm and hip and took refuge in the vacant Russell house.

Bleeding from his wounds and unable to escape from the house surrounded by his armed enemies, he sent a youth to quickly gallop northward to fetch the Sheriff. The outlaw who had for over two years rebelled, fought and snubbed the law now suddenly wanted to surrender and seek the protection of the law.

THE SHERIFF

The lad found the sheriff at his church in Silver Creek, though it was a Saturday. He was doing some repair work in the Sunday School rooms. Dan Lee, a wiry, non-smoking teetotaler, was a staunch Baptist layman and the moderator of the Lawrence County Baptist Association.

He had not aspired to be sheriff but was urged to seek the office by a large group of citizens. He had protested, reminding them that he did not even carry a gun, owned nothing but hunting shotguns and didn't think he could bring himself to shoot anyone. However, his well known integrity and strength of character was just what the law abiding citizens wanted to help quell the rampant lawlessness that had plagued the county since the end of the civil war. He accepted and was easily elected.

When notified that Joe Loftin was wounded and holed up in the Russell house, Lee got one man, Webb Langston, to go with him to bring in Loftin. When Lee arrived at the Russell place, he had Langston to go tell Joe that he was coming in unarmed to talk to him.

Langston came back out and related that Joe said to come on in "but don't try to arrest me." He then entered the house and found Loftin lying in bed with a pistol in hand. He was highly agitated, but through gentle coaxing, Lee was able to get Loftin to agree to return to jail. His choice was apparently not too difficult in view of the armed bounty hunters lurking outside. Joe first insisted on being able to keep his pistol for the ride to Monticello for his protection, but according to Sheriff Lee's later report of the incident he had taken Joe's two long guns and turned them over to two bystanders, R.A. Daniels and Dr. Larkin, and made Joe give him his pistol which he "belted around myself."

The trip to the Monticello jail was apparently uneventful, and Joe was quickly placed in a cell upon arrival in the early evening hours.

However, it didn't take long for word to spread that the notorious killer had been captured and ensconced in the local brig. The next day, a Sunday, angry wads of men milled around the jail. The mood was vicious and ominous. The sheriff had a problem. How could he get this guy out of his jail, safely though the gathering mob and back to the penitentiary in Jackson? There were only two modes of transportation overland then: horses and railroads, and no railroad was yet open to Monticello.

Dan's wife Matt was a spirited woman, a little older than Dan, daughter of confederate veteran Robert Edmondson of Rawls Springs, Mississippi. She was always a great partner to her husband, and she fulfilled her role in this knotty and dangerous problem. On Monday afternoon after she, the sheriff and his handful of deputies had previously planned their strategy, she arrived at the jail yard that was teeming with surly, vengeful, self-appointed vigilantes.

She approached the crowd in her buggy angrily castigating the mob, and slashing right and left with her buggy whip, and snarling, "Get out of my way you scoundrels. You elected my husband sheriff and he's going to do his job. Out of the way!"

Her fury parted the crowd like Moses before the Red Sea.

Later she and Dan suddenly came out of the jail with a frightened Joe Loftin between them. They walked straight to her buggy, staring down the crowd as they came. Without a word or hesitation, they got into the buggy and headed west at full speed.

The deputies were already on their horses and followed along behind the sheriff's rig. Before the angry lynch-hungry mob could react, the entourage had put considerable distance between them. But the mob hastily mounted their horses and in a disorganized pursuit went pell-mell after them. The deputies rode a little more slowly than the buggy, allowing it to gain ground ahead.

The pursuing mob rode furiously after the deputies and kept following all the way to the Illinois Central railroad station in Brookhaven. However, they had not been able to see that the buggy containing their quarry had taken the right hand fork five miles out of

Monticello and had gone straight to the Wesson station on the IC railroad nine miles north of Brookhaven. By the time the mob discovered the ruse, Joe and Mr. & Mrs. Sheriff were comfortably riding a coach to the penitentiary at Jackson.

The penitentiary records show that Joe was registered back behind the walls August 14, 1888.

The would-be lynch mob could not accept this humiliating defeat and felt a powerful need for revenge against the sheriff. When Dan and Matt Lee wearily returned home late that night, they found their house and barn burned to the ground, and their livestock scattered. This cowardly atrocity did not quench the mob's thirst for vengeance. A meeting of some of this crowd was held on the following day, calling themselves a "committee of law abiding citizens," and passed a resolution for publication in the newspaper condemning the sheriff for disarming private citizens to protect a notorious outlaw, and demanding his resignation.

This audacious condemnation of the sheriff for courageously doing his duty brought forth a furious reaction of righteous indignation from the vast majority of Lawrence County citizens, and they held a true mass meeting on August 22nd. Over four hundred citizens signed their names to a powerfully worded resolution supporting and praising the sheriff for his actions as a "true, honest, faithful and Christian gentlemen" and admiring the "manly manner in which he maintained the law by which he is sworn to be governed." The resolution further condemned the "fire fiend" who burned the sheriff's house, and invited the sheriff to call from the citizens of the county a posse whenever he needed them for enforcement of the law.

Joe, now, in August 1888, was back in prison supposedly for life.

NEW ADVENTURES FOR THE FORLORN LAVINIA

Lavinia with two young boys and carrying an unborn third child was left with no means of support. After the Sauls killing and Joe's departure, she was met in the community with cold hostility, which evoked a letter from a neighbor, Henry Smith, demanding that she leave the area.

She managed to make an arrangement in Osyka with one James Rials whereby she could occupy a portion of his big house and operate it as a boarding house. Rials' father, W. E. Rials, claimed to be a doctor and had founded a company called "The Southern Medicine Company," which produced two patented medicines "Rials Lung Balm" and "Indian Liniment."

Shortly after her arrival in this new environment, she became indirectly involved in another murder case, probably the most notorious murder in Pike County history.

THE VARNADO ASSASSINATION

Dr. Rials was an acquaintance of Dr. J.J. Goss, a prominent and highly respected citizen of Osyka. Besides being a practicing

Robert E. Jones

physician, Dr. Goss operated a drug store and general merchandise store, was editor and founder of a newspaper, The Osyka Two States, and was the Mayor of the town as well as a minister of the gospel for two churches.

Dr. Goss had a spirited rivalry with another druggist, F.H. Varnado. On one Saturday night, November 22, 1888, Varnado was assassinated from ambush as he was closing the door of his store in the evening.

A black man, Henry Sheridan, was later convicted of the crime, but he testified that Dr. Rials, on behalf of Dr. Goss, hired him.

In the December preliminary hearing on charges against the three defendants, Sheridan, Goss and Rials, Lavinia testified to having heard conversations between Rials and Goss shortly after the murder, which clearly implicated Dr. Goss in the murder. She swore that Goss tried to persuade Rials to kill the triggerman Sheridan before he could talk and expose their plot. At the trial of Goss in April, Lavinia was scheduled to testify on the 17th but was not able to be present, because, as testified to by Dr. W.M. Wroten, she gave birth to a baby girl on Tuesday, the 16th and was having convulsions on the 17th and barely able to turn over in bed.

It was nine months since James Sauls had been gunned down on her front porch. Her testimony was later introduced in the trial, which was vital to the prosecution.

The defendant's chief attorney, Hiram Cassedy of Brookhaven, called three witnesses from Lawrence County, Henry C. Smith, B.B. Stringer and J.C. Magee, who impeached the testimony of Mrs. Loftin, swearing that her reputation in her community was bad. Crawford Loftin, Joe's brother, had also been subpoenaed for this purpose but was not called to the stand.

Apparently, the jury disregarded Lavinia's testimony completely. The jury acquitted Dr. Goss, vigorously defended by six able attorneys, though the press and the public generally scorned the verdict. The other defendants weren't so lucky, especially poor Sheridan who got the "hemp halter" and was later hanged.

Meanwhile, Joe remained in prison. This time he was kept within the walls of the big prison. His passion for freedom was not stifled however. On June 7, 1891, he attempted another escape, dropping down from the top of the high walls, breaking his leg, and being quickly recaptured. After this, there were no more recorded escape attempts.

Little is known of Joe's prison activities after this. However, it is possible that he had a maturing and mellowing transformation. In any event, it is known that he later showed up as a free man in Oklahoma after the turn of the century. He lived first with one son in west Texas and later with the other in Oklahoma. His grandson, Guy Loftin, remembered him from the early 20's in Oklahoma. Joe related to him an exciting story of how he said he got away from the Mississippi prison.

He said he had been working with a prison work gang on a plantation in the delta and ran away. Bloodhounds were put on his trail, and he killed the first one to reach him with his bare hands, and then made his way to the banks of the Mississippi River and hid in the canebrake until dawn. He then pushed out into the swirling current on a log when he had spotted a steamboat approaching. The boat picked him up and let him ride all the way to New Orleans where he was able to sign on with a freighter headed for Nicaragua in exchange for his labor aboard ship. He said he stayed there and worked for several years until he thought it safe to return to the states. Some family members speculate that he had worked on the Panama Canal, which was then under construction. But in any event, he made his way somehow to Oklahoma by approximately 1905, where he found his son, Ezra, whom he had not seen since he was a small child. Upon confronting Ezra, he ordered him to take off his shirt, and when examining his bare back, pronounced that he was surely his son for "That there scar is where your mammy drapped her corncob pipe down the back of your shirt when you was just a little chap."

MYSTERIOUS RELEASE

Joe had told the other members of the family that his release was the result of his lawyer, A. H. Longino, being elected governor. He claimed to them that "When my lawyer got elected governor he pardoned me provided I would go to the Indian Territory and never return to Mississippi."

The exact circumstances of his release from prison are a mystery. Intense research in the Mississippi archives does not disclose any pardon, nor do they reflect an escape at the period of his release. A somewhat puzzling notation was found on the roster of

1899 near his name, "Discharged May 1899 for conspicuous meritorious conduct" which phrase is used in a statute then in existence, which authorized the Board of Control (the overseeing body for the prison) to release prisoners with specific approval of the governor. The statute reads as follows:

> **3175. meritorious act of convict.**—For a meritorious public service the board of control may commute the sentence of a convict, and for a conspicuously meritorious act of public service may discharge the convict, with a certificate of the fact; but, in either case, the governor must consent thereto.

No other record could be found to verify that this action had been taken by the Board of Control or that Governor Longino had approved such a release, nor was there any record of a normal pardon by him. Longino was not elected governor until November 1899, after a democratic primary victory in August and inaugurated in 1900. Some speculate that the release was actually made after the governor had been elected and that the scribbled notation on the record was inserted after the fact to cover up a surreptitious sub rosa release. Governor Longino was known as a straight and honest man, and this is not consistent with his reputation. Once he had a man abruptly arrested in his office by the capitol police for attempting to bribe him in connection with the contract for construction of the new capitol building. Longino possibly was sympathetic with Loftin since he had defended him in two trials and one appeal to the Supreme Court and had gotten to know him and his family. However, politically it would have been suicide to legally and openly pardon him, for feelings in his home county of Lawrence and surrounding area were still very fierce against Joe Loftin, the notorious murderer and former scourge of the county. The mystery of the circumstances of Joe Loftin's final release from prison will have to be left for the readers to settle. Did he actually do some "conspicuously meritorious act of public service" justifying discharge by the Board of Control which went unrecorded and unreported in the newspapers, or was there an undercover release which was covered up by a backdated notation on the records? Or, did Joe really escape and make his way to central Americas as he told his grandson?

In 1898, R.W. McNair, brother of Joe's lawyer, A.C. McNair, was appointed warden of the Mississippi penitentiary and was serving in that post when Joe's other lawyer, Mr. Longino, was elected governor and the unexplained release of Joe Loftin occurred. This would appear to add credence to the possibility of a somewhat clandestine "pardon" of Joe in line with what he had related to his family.

EPILOGUE

Joe's wife, Lavinia, had fled to Texas shortly after the Varnado murder trials were over and died April 16, 1897, at age 41 in Bellevue, Texas, on her daughter's 8th birthday. Little Myrtle was placed in the Corsicana State Home but later was released to her brother Ezra in September 1902. Oscar Loftin died in 1946; Ezra in

1947 and Myrtle lived to age 89, dying November 26, 1978. Joe claimed he had attended his wife's funeral in 1897 (two years before his release) and in view of his release later for "meritorious conduct," perhaps he was allowed by the prison warden to attend his wife's funeral. Joe lived to the age of 77, expiring April 2, 1931, and is buried in Mayfield Cemetery seven miles north of Erick, Oklahoma.

The Loftin family sued to set aside the deed to Longino and McNair of Joe's interest in the 720 acre Leonard L. Loftin estate and in a round about way were successful—the Court found that Longino and McNair were entitled to 1/6 of the estate, subject, however, to a dower for the widow of a full one third including the house. A sale was ordered of the other 2/3 with the net proceeds to be divided 6 ways, 5 shares to the Loftin children and one to Longino and McNair. However, Plaintiff's attorney was allowed a fee of $92.85 and court costs of $33.35 to be deducted from the sale. It is suspected that the loyal friends of the Loftins attended the sale and discouraged competitive bidding. Crawford Loftin bid $163.50 for the land and found that no one ventured to outbid him. After deducting court costs and plaintiff's attorney fees and the 5/6 to the Loftins, McNair and Longino netted $6.25 for their services. The officer conducting the sale was Sheriff Dan Lee. Of course, Longino and McNair had also received the 80-acre farm of Joe's, which presumably they were able to sell for a fair price.

Sheriff Dan Lee died July 13, 1924, and is buried in the Monticello Masonic Cemetery. His obituary in the Lawrence County Press was glowing in its praise of the man, saying in part,

Robert E. Jones

"If we possessed the power to run the gamut of the English language and used that power to run the scale with all the melody and beauty of an artist's touch, even then we couldn't paint a picture that would do justice to this good man."

THE LAST LEGAL HANGING IN LINCOLN COUNTY

At the February 1902 meeting of the Lincoln County Board of Supervisors, the following order was passed:

> "It is ordered by the Board of Supervisors of Lincoln County, in the State of Mississippi, in accordance with and by order of the Supreme Court of the State of Mississippi, as described in the mandate of said Court of date of January 23, A.D. 1902, that John Sasser, for his crime of the murder of Thomas Lard, be kept in close confinement in the jail of Lincoln County, Mississippi, by the Sheriff of said county until Tuesday, the 11th day of March, A.D. 1902, on which day, between the hours of 11 a.m. and 4 p.m. he, the said John Sasser, shall be by the sheriff of said county, within the enclosure of the said court house yard of said county, in the city of Brookhaven, Mississippi, hanged publicly by the neck until he be dead."

No white man had ever before been hanged in Lincoln County, nor has any other since.

John Sasser at 39 years of age had earned a reputation of a flamboyant, violent man. He was already under indictment for one murder when he was sentenced to be hanged for another.

White residents had committed numerous other murders, and capital convictions obtained, but invariably the governors would honor the petitions for mercy signed by hundreds of citizens (and voters) and would issue a pardon or commute the death sentence to life imprisonment.

In Sasser's case, petitions for commutation signed by over a thousand residents were sent to Governor Longino, but four days before the execution date, the governor expressed sympathy for the family, "but, as governor, with the grave responsibility on me, I feel I must let the law take its course."

The murder for which Sasser was to pay the highest penalty was of Thomas Lard, a saw filer at the Pearl River Lumber Company and a peaceable, mild man, but a heavy drinker. Apparently, Sasser killed Lard with Lard's own pistol with one shot in the forehead. He was found dying on North First Street on a small bridge, and two men were seen running away.

Sasser disappeared the day after the murder but was soon nabbed after Governor Longino offered a $150 reward.

The other party, Tom Pritchard, from Jefferson County had returned to work the next day and was arrested on the job. Pritchard was kept confined in the Hazlehurst jail until the day of the trial. He was the prosecution's prime witness. Newspaper accounts do not give details of Pritchard's testimony at the trial, but apparently, it was damning. The jury returned a guilty verdict after a short deliberation, and Judge Powell handed down the death sentence. The trial and sentence withstood the scrutiny of the Mississippi Supreme Court, and March 11th was ordered as the execution date. Incidentally, two other condemned murderers in the state had their sentences upheld at the same time—one in Jones County and one in Monroe County—and were given the same date for their rendezvous with destiny.

Sheriff Applewhite tried to persuade the Board of Supervisors to rescind the "public" aspect of their order and allow the hanging to take place inside the jail yard before a restricted audience. However, the supervisors felt public exposure of the event might have a deterrent effect on the more frisky members of the county's population, and furthermore, it wouldn't hurt the popularity of the supervisors at the next election.

The sheriff hurriedly constructed the scaffold in the center of the courthouse lawn where it would afford a clear view from most directions. On the night before the execution, the Methodist pastor, Rev. C. W. Crisler, met with the prisoner in his cell and reported that Sasser had been converted and that he had baptized him in his cell. Sasser had been held in the Hinds County jail and was transported to Brookhaven on the day before the execution arriving at 6 a.m., heavily guarded. When the fateful day arrived, some 7,000 public-spirited folks came to view the free, grisly entertainment.

A barbed wire fence some 60 feet square surrounded the scaffold. Inside the enclosure were admitted the supervisors, Dr. Butler, county health doctor, several other physicians, ministers and members of the press while a huge throng surged against the enclosure. Sasser appeared just before two o'clock p.m. manacled, but neat and freshly shaved except for his mustache and wearing a new blue suit.

Methodist Rev. C. W. Crisler and Rev. R. Z. Germany united in singing a stanza, "Oh, How I Love Jesus," then Sheriff Applewhite announced that the condemned man desired to make a statement. No introduction was necessary. The crown hushed and moved closer to hear every word.

Sasser spoke and rambled on for nearly an hour, praising his friends and the sheriff and others who had been kind to him. He raved against his enemies, especially the star witness, Prichard, and the editor of the paper who had lambasted him repeatedly in the paper. He seemed to soften for a moment with assurance of forgiveness and hoped he would meet the editor in "The Sweet Bye and Bye."

He expressed a strong regard for his family and boasted that he had never mistreated his wife nor struck one of his children and had never ridden his horse into the house and hitched him to the bed post, like some people do.

In the crowd was Frank H. Hartman, Sr., who had a running feud with Sasser, the cause of which no one seemed to know. According to an account by Oscar Hartman, Jr., a grandson, as published in Gil Hoffman's <u>Dummy Lines Through the Longleaf</u> book, Sasser spotted Hartman in the mob and called out to him, "You better go and look after your mill, Hartman, I believe it's burning from all four corners about now." A thin plume of black smoke could be seen rising over the southwest horizon at the time. Undaunted, Hartman shouted back, "Let the damn mill burn, I'm going to stay here and watch you take your last jerk!" Which he did, and his mill

Mississippi Gumbo

was destroyed by fire, undoubtedly by Sasser's last vicious conspiracy.

Then Sasser began to taper off in his remarks, magnanimously forgiving everyone in the audience. Then, as most good speakers do, he asked if there were any questions. He wasn't prepared for the straightforward query, which shot back at him loud and clear, "Did you kill Tom Lard?"

Sasser appeared rattled and stammered, "I've already stated that. I believe that is all I want to say."

The ministers sang another hymn, "Jesus, Lover of My Soul," and Sheriff Applewhite adjusted the noose around Sasser's neck. Sasser then shook hands with everyone in the enclosure and bade them farewell. Marshall Applewhite adjusted the black cap over Sasser's face, and all was ready.

Sheriff Applewhite sprung the trap, and the condemned man's body dropped suddenly seven feet through the opening. There was no visible twitch or movement from the body. It was instant death, and he was promptly pronounced dead. His neck was broken.

The crowd, subdued, slowly and silently filtered away.

HOME TOWN LYNCHINGS

When one writes about history, in order to be objective and complete there must be recorded not only the proud, thrilling and positive events, but also the shameful and disgraceful occurrences. Brookhaven is as fine a community as can be found, but it has its dark side in the past that should not be swept under the rug. It must be remembered, recorded and acknowledged to purge the conscious of the community.

Two of these abhorrent chapters come to mind.

As reported by the New Orleans papers and from details in Herman Dean's memoirs, on December 27, 1907, outside of Ruth (a village twenty miles southeast of Brookhaven) a black man named Eli Pigott brutally sexually assaulted a white girl and fled into Louisiana through Pike County. Early in November, another black man named Bob Ashley shot and killed the marshal of Oakvale, a village in Lawrence County, some twelve miles south of Monticello.

The marshal had undertaken to arrest him believing him to be Pigott. He wounded the suspect, but Ashley escaped and showed up the next day in Brookhaven where he went to a black physician to have his severe wound dressed. The doctor notified the sheriff who formed a small posse, and they went a-hunting. They received a tip that such a man was hiding in a small house in the sawmill quarters of Pearlhaven. The posse surrounded the house and captured the man.

On his way to jail, a crowd of some 30 or 40 angry men from Lawrence and Lincoln Counties intercepted the posse, forcibly tore the suspect loose from his captors, and shot him to death. His body was put in the jail overnight, and it was only then determined that the dead man was Ashley of Lawrence County and not Eli Pigott.

Later Pigott appeared in Kentwood, Louisiana, and was identified. The Louisiana sheriff took him to the parish jail in New Orleans. He was kept there until the Circuit Court Judge in Lincoln County called a special term of court for a trial, and an elaborate plan was then worked out with the Mississippi National Guard. Louisiana officers took him to Jackson, Mississippi, for safekeeping. On the first day of the special term of court, the manacled Pigott was put on the New Orleans limited train escorted by a company of National Guard troops from Jackson and by Lincoln County's sheriff and two deputies. They were to be met at the Brookhaven station by a company of the local guard. They felt that surely this was sufficient force to deliver the prisoner to the court.

In the meanwhile, a special train on the Natchez, Columbia, and Mobile Railroad (the Butterfield Lumber Company railroad) had been arranged for by the father of the assault victim and was chugging from Ruth to Norfield packed to the gills with outraged men. It was timed to connect with the local IC train going north to Brookhaven.

Train No. 1, on which the prisoner and his guard were to arrive, was ten to fifteen minutes late when it reached Brookhaven. This threw it behind the arrival of the local train from the south, which was loaded with resolute men from south Lincoln County, and a large crowd from the immediate vicinity where the crime had been perpetrated.

When they arrived a few minutes before the train from Jackson and saw the Brookhaven soldiers already drawn up in line armed with rifles with bayonets, the determined men conjured up in their minds that Pigott might in some way escape speedy justice under military protection. They decided to take no chances and resolved to seize Pigott at all costs before he reached the jail and to make short work of him.

Their first onslaught was made before the prisoner and all of the Jackson military company had fairly alighted from the train. The attackers soon were able to get their hands on Pigott. He was cut two or three times, given several blows on the head, and thrown to the ground before the guard could beat back the assault and make a start for the jail. Then the soldiers, led by the sheriff holding to his prisoner with his left hand and brandishing a big forty-four in his right, started southward along the railroad at a quick pace headed for the jail.

The angry mob followed in hot pursuit, increasing in number as bystanders joined it and by the time the prisoner and his guard had left the railroad, and turned east up Chickasaw Street toward the jail, it had swelled to a crowd of one thousand strong, completely blocking the way of the sheriff and soldiers. At this point, the Ruth group was further reinforced by a large number of locals who had previously gathered near the jail to prevent Pigott from being admitted.

When the soldiers were brought to a halt the second time by the angry, determined mob, the father of the girl broke through the line to get to Pigott. In so doing, he received two heavy blows on his head from a gun in the hands of a young soldier and caught a third blow from a bayonet, lacerating his head. Just at this moment, someone threw a noose over Pigott's neck; and ready hands caught the trailing end of the halter, dragged Pigott from the soldiers and the sheriff, and forced him back toward the railroad crossing. As soon as the massive gang had gotten full possession of the prisoner, they began firing into him as they hustled him along, riddling him with scores of shots.

When Pigott, now dead, was dragged across to the west side of the railroad by the excited rabble-rousers, volley after volley was fired into his body as the crowd yelled like demons. The shouts and cries of the demented throng seemed to come straight from hell. After Pigott was dragged up against the curbing of the sidewalk, and even though all evidence of life was extinct, some of the more ghoulish members of the mob continued to attack and mutilate the bodily remains of the victim.

Among the very last of the maniacal avengers to come up at this time and fire a volley into the prostrate and lifeless body was the enraged father who had sufficiently recovered from the stunning blows he had received from the soldiers. Several members of the mob then seized the rope and dragged the victim's body to an electric light pole in front of where the funeral home now sits. One member quickly scaled the pole and fastened the rope over one of the foot pegs, and the body of Eli Pigott was quickly hoisted eight or ten feet from the ground and left dangling in plain view of the immense crowd which had by this time gathered in sight of the scene.

The perpetrators of this heinous exhibition, their blood lust now satiated, began to disperse. At first, they pranced away with an air of triumphant and victory; but as they glanced at the unnerved peaceful citizens silently gazing open-mouthed at the scene in disbelief, it seemed as though second thoughts were beginning to creep into their consciousness as they lowered their heads.

TWENTY YEARS LATER

On June 29, 1928, there occurred a vicious and ghastly double lynching in the "Home Seekers' Paradise." Two black brothers had gotten in an altercation with the owners of a car repair shop located across from where the library is now situated. In the conflict, the brothers had shot the business owners, one receiving a shattered leg bone. Deputy Charles Brister captured one of the blacks at the scene, but the other assailant had a running gun battle with police as he retreated northwardly towards the old compress area on North First Street.

The police chief, J. Walter Smith, and Sheriff Martin J. Brister knew his identity and went immediately to his residence. He was found hiding in a closet. A bulldog that had been trained by Cecil Mathis let the officers know where he was. Knowing the subject was armed and ready to defend himself, the officers opened the door a small amount and commanded the dog to "Sic 'em!" which he immediately did and shots came out of the closet whereupon the officers opened up with all they had into the closet door. The officers and the dog escaped unhurt, but five bullets hit the cowering fugitive. He was arrested, taken to the jail and put in the cell with his brother and another man whom the officers thought was an accomplice. Dr. Frizzell, the county health doctor, was called to assess the condition of the bullet-ridden subject. He dressed the wounds and pronounced the inmate in no danger from them.

News of the event spread throughout the county and by late afternoon, the area of the jail and courthouse were teeming with angry whites and curious excitement seekers. Soon the crowd began to organize and plan their action, at the same time sharing drinks of hard liquor among themselves. It was not long before some of them obtained an 8" by 8" timber ten feet long to batter the jail doors. They faced the seemingly daunting task of getting past the sheriff and other leading citizens and three steel doors to reach their prey. Several prominent citizens, including T. Brady, Jr., W. D. Davis, Mayor P. Z. Jones and J. A. Naul pleaded with them to desist and to let the law take its course, but their pleas were no match to the whisky-fueled rage of the mad men. Sheriff Brister faced the rabble and physically attempted to block the entrance, receiving a badly hurt forearm from the ramming timber. It took only two hours for the three steel doors to give way to the furious ramming. They hauled the two brothers away in separate automobiles, turning the third suspect loose. By this time, there were about forty automobiles lined up in front of the jail headed south. Shouts of "Ole Brook! Ole Brook!" rang out as the red-eyed vigilantes set out on their course to the original site of Brookhaven.

Upon arrival at the Ole Brook Bridge, they found a suitable tree; and after putting a noose around one of the poor victim's neck, they threw the other end over a strong limb. Someone shouted: "No shootin' 'til he's dead!" which was obeyed, but it didn't take long for the grim reaper to collect his bounty. Then the jubilant participants enthusiastically emptied their firearms into the lifeless body.

For an encore, the imaginative group put a rope around the other victim's neck, but instead of finding a tree for him, they rode to the edge of town and then tied the rope to the rear axle of the car and forced him to follow along behind as they slowly drove through town. The pitiful prey was allowed to keep pace with the car for a short while; but at one point, he managed to catch up to the car and jumped onto its spare tire, but was brutally kicked off. The driver then gradually increased the speed until he could no longer keep up, stumbled, and was dragged by his neck through the city for about a half hour until the lynchers lost their zest for the sport since it was apparent that no more pain could be inflicted on the victim.

They then headed up old Highway 51 about five miles and turned off near Clear Branch Church where the remainder of the body was hauled up a tree on the creek and left for all to see.

Sheriff Brister called Hartman's Funeral Home to take down the bodies, and they had the two lying side by side in the morgue before midnight. Their joint funeral was held the next day at New

Robert E. Jones

Hope church five miles northwest of town. No charges were ever filed for the killings.

THE AMERICAN DO NUTHIN PARTY CONVENTION

Excerpts from the transcript of the recent national convention of the Do Nuthin Party, which nominated Senator (Ret.) J. Greyfeather Beauregard to lead their ticket for president in the 2004 election, are presented herewith:

INTRODUCTION OF NOMINEE OF DO NUTHIN PARTY
By: Stonewall J. Thudpucker

I am here to introduce a great patriot. A valiant Galahad of Golden Heart, with soul as unblemished as the creamy purity of winter's first snow. A man of courage as fiery as hell's fury; a champion with honor as perfect as the ring of a silver bell at a spring sunrise; a gentlemen with compassion as tender as a child's heart-rending teardrop for his slain dog.

Yea, I say unto you that here is a genius whose thoughts soar in the heavens as the eagle's flight above the great yawning canyon. Here is a compassionate soul whose heart pounds for his fellow being as the Pacific surf crashes upon the craggy rocks. Here is a saint in armor whose soul pines for perfection just as the pure hearted bride longs for her groom. (Pause)

Why, lo, his rich bugled voice has continually echoed in clarion tones the call for patriotism through the halls of time. His trumpet of challenge to all foes of liberty has reverberated through the black forest of ignorance with the audacity of the bulk elk heroically daring all opponents.

(Forcefully) His valor and gallantry on all issues are badges of red courage to be displayed with unequalled pride on the breasts of his constituents throughout all the age.

(Pause) (Softly-tenderly) And at last when upon some distant color-splashed sunset, he finally lays to rest his crimson stained rapier of morality and rectitude, his battered but shining shield of honesty, truth and valor will be hung in a place of honor in the Valhalla of the brave knights who have fought the good fight, the divine fight, the gallant fight, in quest of the right, the pure, the noble; then tears of love will drench his grave and thence spring to life, blossoms of the sweetest nectar ever sipped and of the loveliest hues ever glimpsed. And upon the spot will be raised a monument of gleaming marble, rising above all others, as he towered over all in life; and upon it shall be inscribed in letters of gleaming gold for all to see, "Here lies Liberty's greatest champion."

I present to you J. Greyfeather Beauregard!

ACCEPTANCE ADDRESS

Senator Beauregard: Thank you, thank you, Judge Thudpucker for those simple but kind words. We are so glad that the Judge was able to be with us today. He has been a shut-in for quite some time now, but finally his long awaited and well-deserved parole has been granted.

It is with great humility that I again accept the nomination of this great party for the highest office this great nation has to offer.

At the last election, we made many mistakes that we will strive to avoid this time. We were able to get on the ballot of only Haiti but then to be advised that Haiti is not yet a state. But this time we'll be ready.

Since then, a ground swell of support has spontaneously erupted like lava bursting forth from the mighty volcano Mt. Everest.

You know why we are getting stronger. The crown of thorns of too many laws and regulations is being pressed down upon the brow of the hard working taxpaying citizens of this great civilization.

We must put a stop to it. Here is our Platform. (Displays blank sheet of paper). Yes, it's blank, we will not pass any laws when we get control of the government. The Populace will be freed of carrying the heavy cross of taxation and regulations. The people will rejoice and dance in the streets. We will be the most popular administration since Washington was elected in 1492.

But we've got a fight on our hands. The scions of greed and power will not give any quarter or even a penny. We will fight them in the cities, in the country, in the streets, on the beaches in the hills and valleys. We will never surrender. When we win and should our party last for a thousand years, it will be said, "This was their Finest Hour."

The long gray line has never failed us, but should we falter in this great crusade, then millions of ghosts in blue, gray, khaki shall rise up to haunt us with cries of Duty, Honor, and Party. And the day we lose will be a day that shall live in infamy.

We have nothing to fear but fear itself. Never have so many owed so little to so few. I have nothing to offer but Blood, Toil, Tears and Sweat.

I had a dream. I have been to the mountaintop and seen the Promised Land where little democrats, republicans and Do Nuthin'ers play peacefully and freely with one another.

Ask not what Beauregard can do for you, but what you can do for Beauregard!

I ACCEPT THE NOMINATION.

I promise we will do nuthin, but we will do nuthin right!

However, there is one program I shall institute. You know the two greatest problems of our Southland are the costly pine beetle and the destructive fire ants. I am assured from my scientific advisers that something can be done. I propose to appropriate five hundred million dollars for research to develop a pine beetle that eats nothing but fire ants - - then when they've eaten all the fire ants, the pine beetles will die of starvation.

Thank you, thank you, and calm down now…

HALLELUJAH! DO NUTHIN!

And now Judge Thudpucker will lead us in our campaign song.

Mississippi Gumbo

BEAUREGARD CAMPAIGN SONG

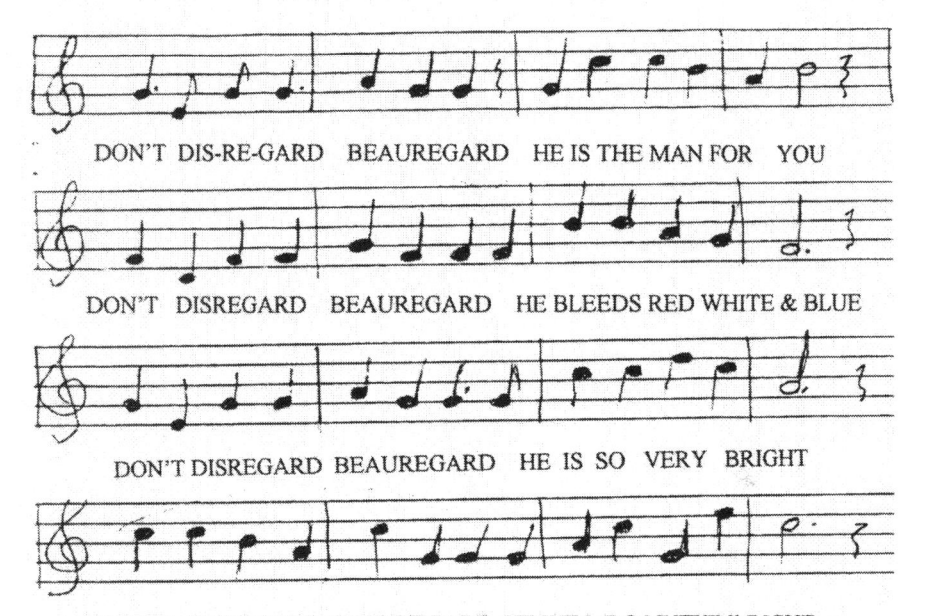

DON'T DIS-RE-GARD BEAUREGARD HE IS THE MAN FOR YOU

DON'T DISREGARD BEAUREGARD HE BLEEDS RED WHITE & BLUE

DON'T DISREGARD BEAUREGARD HE IS SO VERY BRIGHT

DON'T DISREGARD BEAUREGARD HE WILL DO NUTHIN' RIGHT

Second Verse: Don't Disregard Beauregard His Character Is Strong
Don't Disregard Beauregard He Won't Do Any Wrong
Don't Disregard Beauregard To Him We All Must Cling
Don't Disregard Beauregard He Won't Do Anything.

CHORUS

DO NUTHIN' DO NUTHIN' THE PARTY WILL GO FAR

DO NUTHIN' DO NUTHIN' JUST LEAVE IT LIKE IT ARE!

GREAT THINGS TO PONDER

Do you ever ponder? Some people never do—they just go through life without caring or considering the deep mystifying puzzles of the universe. I ponder a lot.

For example, how long will a bar of soap last? Does anyone know? Have you ever completely used one up? No—nobody has. (Except my wife who claims to have used them to the last lather, but I never have put much stock in what she says regarding matters of pure science or philosophy.) When it gets down to a thin sliver, you just throw it away. I am currently running a test to see how long it takes for a bar of soap to completely vanish. I have two slivers, one in my shower and one in the bathroom sink. The bathroom sliver is down to about 1/8 of an inch thick—while the other is down to approximately 3/32 of an inch. I think the shower one will disappear first, but I won't have any witnesses. The shower one is 47 days old, and the sink one is only 38 days old. Something to ponder.

How about those packs of 300 Q-tips—little plastic sticks with a wad of cotton on each end. You know how much they sell for? Guess, well—it's $1.00 per box. 300 Q-tips for $1.00! How can they do this? I can see the poor little oriental girls sitting at a bench, taking the plastic sticks and swirling some cotton on each end. How long would it take to do one stick perfectly? Probably at least 15 seconds after much practice—that's 4 per minute—240 per hour—so 300 Q-tips would take over an hour of labor. What's the pay rate? 20 cents per hour? Ok, that's about 25 cents labor for each box. Materials? The sticks and cotton and the packaging? Could you get 300 little sticks and the cotton at 10 for a penny and package it? I doubt it—but ok, that now runs the cost up to 55 cents total. What about the factory overhead, the management, utilities, etc.—Can the factory come out selling wholesale at 15 cents markup to cover overhead and profit? I doubt it, but now that's 70 cents when it leaves the factory. Then there's transportation to a port—5 cents; transportation over the 6000 miles to the West Coast—at least 10 cents, now it's up to 85 cents. Unloading by teamsters and delivery by truck to a wholesaler - 5 cents. So, the wholesaler gets its for 90 cents, he adds at least 5% or 4 ½ cents to the price—now it 94 ½ cents. He ships it to drug store chains—with sales commission and more transportation another 10% - now it's at $1.03 delivered to the store. So, I guess the discount drug store's got to be losing money. How do they do it? Well, It's something to ponder.

Moving right along, I've pondered over gasoline mileage and the cost per mile in our car. That's relatively simple to compute. If you fill your tank after driving 240 miles, and it takes 15 gallons, and the price is $1.09 per gallon, all you have to do is...—Well, you do the math. Once some of us guys went fishing down in Mexico.— There we drove 320 kilometers one day; and when we filled up, it took 15.5 liters of gasoline at a cost of 249 pesos. If the exchange rate was 15 pesos to the dollar, how much did it cost in dollars per mile? Again, you do the math. Had enough pondering?

Often times, directions in recipes or on medicine have to be carefully pondered. One of my prescriptions requires me to "take one capsule twice a day." This caused me pause. I reasoned that if they wanted me to take two capsules every day, they would have said so, but no, they said to take <u>one</u> capsule <u>twice</u> a day. This is somewhat of a problem. I swallow it once, but I have the dickens of a time getting it back up to take it again.

Also, a recipe for egg drop soup says, that after bringing the soup to a boil and dropping the well-beaten egg into it, you should then cook it "slowly for one minute." If they give you a specific time limit, why say "slowly?" Is there a difference in cooking it "quickly" for one minute and cooking it "slowly" for one minute. I couldn't ponder that one out. I went on and cooked it for a minute but wasn't sure whether it was a quick minute or a slow one.

Sometimes you have to ponder what people say to you. The other day when I sat down in the chair of a new barber, I was politely asked if I wanted "it cut above your ears." This requires some serious pondering since I have hardly any hair—below my ears. I didn't think it would be an imposition for her to cut my hair that lies above my ears, so I told the young lady, "Yes, please cut my hair above my ears since that is where most of it is located." I really thought she would have picked up on that on her own, but anyway it took some pondering.

Once I spent about a week at my cabin on a lake, and it brought new appreciation of many things and stimulated my pondering. The predawn meditation and study was soul cleansing.

Several mornings just before the sunrise, I walked down to the pier and cast a lure a few times to hopefully snare a bass. The pier has a square platform at the end with benches and an iron railing with an opening at one point to allow stepping into or out of a boat. I would stand in front of this opening to cast my fishing lure. Before standing, I would brush away a spider web, which stretched across the opening. On the third morning of this practice, I was struck by the realization that this delicate and beautiful spider web had been reconstructed across this opening each day. Rather than swipe it aside, I studied it. Its pattern was exquisite. Strands from the tops of each side post extended downward to the lower portion of the other vertical post, and the intricate maze extended out to cover most of the opening between the side posts. I marveled at it. How did the spider get it started? How could he attach one end of a tiny "cable" and get across to the other post to tie it there? Did he swing across like a Tarzan? Did he go all the way down to the floor and then crawl up the other post? How could he do this? When I finally located the little creature on one of the posts, he looked nothing more than a few twisted microscopic wires. I couldn't even see any eyes on him. He hung around one side of the web, in contact with a strand. Apparently, when he felt the movement of a struggling insect caught in his trap, he would spring to action and devour it.

As I mulled over these wonders, the sun was rising behind me, I turned to face the coming brilliance, and there in the other side of the pier was another web, woven even more intricately than the one I had been studying. This was lit up by the sun's rays, the strands appeared as tiny neon lights, and the web was exquisite in its beauty. I gazed intently, appreciating nature's wonders.

The next morning when I went down to fish, I did my casting over the rail. I nodded "Good morning" to my spider friends and did not destroy their marvelous works. I hope they appreciated my restraint.

THE TRAGEDY OF PEGGY O'NEAL

CAST

<u>Singing Narrator</u> in front of stage.

Characters who Pantomime everything Narrator says:
Characters:
        Peggy O'Neal   An innocent young girl
        Bill Bailey   A dapper glib swashbuckler
        Mother and Father   Typical rural parents
        Strangers in street   A couple passing by
        Whistling Postman   Young single man who's quite a whistler

Prior to opening "curtain," usher quietly places boxes of Kleenex in spots convenient for audience.

Soft piano music in background tinkly, old-fashioned tunes.

<u>STAGE:</u>

One side of stage represents the old homestead—couch and rocking chair. The other side has two tables with checkered cloths and several chairs—representing a tavern.

Robert E. Jones

OPENING SCENE:

Peggy, Mama, and Papa sitting in living room, Peggy sewing, Mama knitting, and Papa reading paper.

NARRATOR:

Once there was a lovely young girl named Peggy O'Neal, living happily with her mother and father in a small southern town.

She had lived a pure sheltered life, never having been courted by any suitor since her father was very strict and said she could receive a caller only after she was 22.

There was also a young dapper traveling salesman who came to town often. He had seen Peggy several times, as she hung out the washing and fed the pigs. He had fallen madly in love with this young maiden though they had never met.

But he used to describe her to his friends who would inquire as to what she was like

-----SONG-----by Narrator

If her eyes are Blue as Skies that's my little Peggy O'Neal.
If she's smiling all the while, that's my Peggy O'Neal.
If she walks like a sly little Rogue; if she talks with a cute little brogue,
Sweet personality full of Rascality,
That's Peggy O'Neal.
(To the surprise of Narrator, the cast rushes up to echo in harmony the last line "That's Peggy O'Neal!")

Mississippi Gumbo

NARRATOR:

Bill is determined to meet Peggy. He knocks on the door ("ding dong" by prop man)—(Narrator eyes prop man) and is admitted by Peggy. He charms Peggy with his smooth talk. He compliments her hair, her eyes, blue as skies, her beauty, her smile, her brogue, her walk, and her personality. He professes great love for her. He proposes marriage, on bended knee. She is captivated completely. They go out arm in arm laughing before her shocked parents who object strenuously.

The young lovers decide to get married right away. Bill gives her a silver goblet for a gift, Peg gives him a very fine-toothed comb, and they settle down in a little apartment.

(Parents exit stunned.)

However, the sweet little love nest was short lived. Bill's drinking increased; he was unfaithful and lost his job. He spent most of his money on whisky, women, gambling, and wasted all the rest. Peggy could stand it no longer. One raining evening, she put him out with nothing but his fine toothcomb.

She was alone and frightened, but her pride would not allow her to return to her home, so she went to the big city to make her own way.

But times were hard, and she had to do whatever she had to do to get by.

She would even beg on the street corners.

Robert E. Jones

People would pass by and say: (Peggy standing holding silver goblet and begging—

People passing by snubbing her.)

----SONG----

She is more to be pitied than censured.

She is more to be helped than despised.

She is only a lassie who ventured,

Down life's stormy path ill-advised.

Do not scorn her with words,

fierce and bitter.

Do not laugh at her shame and downfall for a moment just stop and consider that a man was the cause of it all!

(Cast comes up behind Narrator and joins in harmony:)

THAT A MAN WAS THE CAUSE OF IT ALLLLL!

(ALL POINT TO BILL)

NARRATOR:

Then one fine day, Peggy got a letter. There was a loud knock at the door ("ding dong!") (Narrator glares at prop man.) **It was whistling postman with a letter, a letter edged in black!** (He is whistling melody of "I Wonder Who's Kissing Her Now." Postman is ATTRACTED to Peggy - - very sympathetic about the Letter.)

(Postman and Peggy pantomime the action of the song.)

Mississippi Gumbo

----SONG----

(Narrator)

Letter Edged in Black

I could hear the Postman whistling yesterday morning,
Coming up the pathway with his pack,
But he little knew the sorrow that he brought me,
As he handed me a Letter Edged in Black.
I opened the door and took the Letter from him.
I broke the seal and this is what it said:
Come Home my dear your poor old mother wants you.
Please come home my child your dear old Daddy's dead.
The last words your dear old father uttered,
Were tell my Peg I wish she would come back.
My eyes are dim my poor old heart is breaking,
As I write to you this Letter Edged in Black.

(Cast gathers to echo in harmony "Edged in Black.")

NARRATOR:

Peggy quickly packed her meager belongings and sold her silver goblet to the Postman to buy a bus ticket home.

Back in the old homestead with mother - one day while Peg is busy in the kitchen, Mama hears the doorbell. ("KNOCK, KNOCK") (Prop man gets another **glare** from Narrator.) **It's Bill! He comes in but is met with a blistering glare from Mama. He pleads with Mama. He wants Peggy to come back to him. He's quit_drinking.** (Bill pantomimes everything said.) **He's quit**

gambling. He's got a job. Bought a new suit, new shoes, gotten his teeth fixed. Getting nowhere, Bill turns on the charm. He compliments Mama—beautiful home, so neat and clean; loves her new hair-do, (no response) **her new dress, her even temper.** (still nothing but steely glare) **He begs on bended knee, both knees. He grovels on the floor.** (Actor playing Bill rebels, refuses to grovel on floor, firing mental daggers at Narrator, stands up to face Mama.) **Mama's mind is made up. Finally she speaks...**(awkward pause, she's forgotten her lines)

(Narrator cues her with each line of song.)

----SONG----

Narrator (Sotto Voice)	She was happy 'till she met you.
Mama	She was happy 'till she met you.
Narrator	And the fault is all your own.
Mama	And the fault is all your own.
Narrator	If she wishes to forget you, you will please leave her alone.
Mama	If she wishes to forget you, you will please leave her alone.
Narrator	She had come to her (hic! - Excuse me) old mother.
Mama	She had come to her (hic! - Excuse me) old mother.
Narrator	You're so stupid.
Mama—(singing)	You're so stupid.
Narrator	Just because there is no other.
Mama	Just because there is no other.
Narrator	She'll be happy in her own sweet home.
Mama	She'll be happy in her own sweet home.

Cast Joins In
Her own Sweet Home!!

NARRATOR:

Bill went away his heart rent in twain. Mother never told Peg that he had come.

(Scene—two tables with chairs,—tavern accouterments. Bill is sitting at table stage left facing off to the left. As he begins song, Peggy and the Postman enter and sit at other table, facing opposite direction from Bill)

NARRATOR:

Years later—Bill sitting alone in a distant tavern could be heard saying to himself:

------SONG----- by Bill

(Postman whistles along with song)
Oh, I wonder who's kissing her now
I wonder who's showing her how
I wonder who's looking into her eyes
Breathing Sighs Telling Lies
I wonder who's buying her wine
For lips that I used to call mine, and I wonder if she ever tells him of <u>me</u>
I wonder who's kissing her now

Robert E. Jones

Cast echoes in harmony "KISSING HER NOW!

VOICE OFF STAGE: "HER <u>WHAT</u>?

<u>NARRATOR</u>:

Back at the old homestead Peggy cried her self to sleep every night saying:

FINALE

ENTIRE CAST

----SONG----

<u>First time through tenderly and sadly by Peggy</u> (or <u>may</u> be recited by Peg rather than Sung)

Won't you come home Bill Bailey

Won't you come home

She moans the whole nightlong

I'll do the cooking Baby

I'll pay the rent

I know I've done you wrong

'Member that Rainy Night

When I put you out

With nothing but a fine tooth comb

I know I'm to blame

Well ain't dat a shame

Bill Bailey won't you please

Come Home.

SECOND TIME

SONG REPEATED BY ENTIRE CAST WITH SLOWLY INCREASING GUSTO AND TEMPO (EXCEPT BILL WHO IS OFF STAGE)

THIRD TIME

SONG REPEATED AGAIN WITH ENTHUSIASM AND DANCING, PRANCING BY WHOLE CAST AS BILL ENTERS, EMBRACES PEGGY AND JOINS IN, PLAYING TRUMPET. ALSO, ENTERING STAGE AND JOINING IN ARE A CLARINET PLAYER, A TROMBONE PLAYER AND A TUBA, OR WHATEVER! ALSO MAYBE MAJORETTES WITH BATONS, ETC.

CURTAIN

CONVERSATION WITH AN ALIEN

Where are you really from!?

Just as I've tried to tell you, I'm from what you call "outer space". A group of us have been here for quite a while studying your civilization, technology, language, anatomy, so forth.

I'm not sure if I believe you—why would you study our <u>anatomy</u>—you are just like us—you are just like a normal human being.

Well, thank you, that's a compliment. We tried to reach a form as identical to you as we could. We weren't sure if we'd be able to fool humans.

Where are you from? How'd you get here?

We're from a planetary system in your own galaxy, about 35 light years away. Naturally we couldn't actually be transported physically that far, even at the speed of light. No one would care to spend that much time on a boring space trip. We, and our space ship, you may call it, were disintegrated on our planet and reconstituted here. It's done by sending our negative cosmic image to a space station near our planet and sending our positive image to another space station located in the other direction. Then the two images are transmitted simultaneously towards your sun and aimed to intersect in your solar system. Where they intersect, we become reconstituted. I don't really

understand it, it's out of my field, but, in effect, we were reconstituted here simultaneously (at least as close to simultaneously as technically possible) as when we were disintegrated. It sure beats poking along for years at the speed of light.

Wow!! How'd you know we were here?

We had been sending out radio wave interceptors for a long time and we got some positive reading from this area.

How long?

Well, in your time frame, about 200,000 years, and we recently started picking up signals. We've been sending observers for about ten years, your time.

Well, we've been seeing flying saucers since the early 50's. That's over thirty years.

Yes, there have been observers from other places here before us.

Other places?

Yes, at least two others. They're rivals of ours, not enemies, but rivals. They're from a place farther away than we are and, well, I'd rather not get into that, highly classified, you know.

Gosh! What do you want here? Are you going to attack us or invade?

Gracious no! We are simply interested in studying your culture and your development—just like you study animals, plants, bacteria, and primitive peoples. Oh we may want to

Mississippi Gumbo

maintain a base here, or station to study you, or for further travel in the area.

You said you have been listening for radio signals for 200,000 years? My goodness, how old is your civilization?

Well we reached approximately the stage of your present development about 300,000 years ago, your time. Before that, I'm not sure how old we were.

Well, what do you think of us?

Very interesting. You plodded along for several thousand years making very little progress then in the last 100 years you have been astounding in your rapid advancement. Your technological development has been phenomenal. That's why we are here; we enjoy watching other worlds develop. We prefer to remain anonymous and be unobserved so as not to give you any help in your advancement. As soon as you solve your economic, environmental, disease problems, and the interrelations problems, you know, wars, race, rivalries, etc., you will really begin to advance with improvements in your bodies and your living. That's the exciting part.

Improvements in our bodies? What kind of improvements?

Well, things like stabilizing your bodies at age 26 or thereabouts, of course, population has to be controlled first. Learning to exist outside your body, changing the size, strength, shape, appearance of your body at will, living forever, getting a new body when you need one, etc. Transporting your ego—spirit anywhere at will. Things like that...

How can you get a new body?

That certainly shouldn't be difficult for you to understand. Your medical world has been into transplanting organs, heart, liver, lungs, etc. for quite some time. Eventually you'll be going for the whole ball of wax.

Wait a minute! How could you get an <u>entire</u> new body all at once? You wouldn't be the same person—what happens to the old body?

Well, you don't get an <u>entirely</u> new body.

Ah Ha! I thought so!

You have to save one little piece to maintain your identity.

What piece?

What would you say makes you <u>you</u>? What makes you an individual? Where is your ego located?

Must be the brain—

The brain is largely a mechanism that performs functions for the body, the clearinghouse and control center for all bodily activity. You could substitute the frontal lobes of another person and maybe improve your thinking ability, but you would still be you. You could transplant the large part of the cerebrum that handles motor actions, and you're still you.

We could literally transplant about 99% of the brain mass from another person into your head and throw away 99% of your brain, and you'd still be you, that is, if we left you with the proper 1% - that 1% of the brain—a section about the size of a peanut—contains the—what?

I don't know—the Soul?

Well, maybe it does, but I doubt that's the physical location of your "soul".

What then?

It's simply your memory. Your recollection of all of your experiences from before birth to the present. As long as you've got that, you're you.

Aw—that doesn't make sense!

Think about it. If we took your peanut sized memory out of your brain and swapped it with that of Charlie Bates, which would you be? When your old body woke up, it would have the complete memory, skills, education, and training of Charlie Bates. If you asked that body or person who he was he would say, "I'm Charlie Bates" and "How in the hell did I get into this body?" When you lay in bed coming out of the anesthetic, you may be dreaming and remembering your past life. Reliving in your mind your earlier accomplishments, thinking of your childhood sweetheart, or doing some mental calculations concerning some business deal you were working on. Then you would begin to come out of the deep sleep. You'd remember going to the operating room and being put to sleep. You'd look at your hands, "Gosh, my hands have sure gotten heavy!" You'd feel your face—it would feel very funny—you'd look down at your legs—they wouldn't be the same as they used to be. Finally, you'd get a mirror and see in the mirror the face of Charlie Bates! But it's still you inside because you remember all of your life. You're

inside! **You may not be able to do all the physical and mental skills you used to do—or you may do some better, but it's you inside. You could visit Charlie Bates' room and get a good look at what you used to look like—even talk with your old body—now Charlie Bates, but you would have no doubt that you- the Real you—was inside the old Charlie Bates' body. It might be fun to challenge your old body to a game of golf or tennis, HA!**

Wait a minute. What about religion? What about our souls? Do we have souls—eternal souls? Is there a God? What about Jesus Christ? Is what He taught real and correct?

Wait a minute yourself. That's one reason we do not like to fraternize, so to speak, with humans. First of all, it's obvious that we know a lot more than you about the universe, and naturally, you know that and will respect what we say. However, we <u>may</u> or <u>may not</u> actually know for sure, the answers to those questions. If we did know the true answer to, say, for instance, the questions of: Is there a God and is Jesus Christ his son? Should we and would we tell you? If the answer is <u>yes</u> and we told you so, we would be interfering with God's plan. You are supposed to decide for yourself, not rely on some outer space traveler. You wouldn't get much credit from upstairs if you believed only because we told you.

On the other hand, if the answers were NO—and we told you, it would be devastating to some of you and others wouldn't believe us anyway.

So—we have to decline to answer any religious questions on the grounds it might tend to interfere with your development. I <u>will</u> say that you can count on a universal law of right and wrong or good and evil and the positive overwhelming power of love. From where that originated, you will just have to decide for yourself.

Now, if you'll excuse me, I've got a call in the spacecraft from home. Have a nice day.

A HAND TO REMEMBER

In the game of bridge, one rarely, if ever, sees a deal with all thirteen cards of one suit in one hand. The odds are roughly 159 billon to one that any of four players will get such a hand on any one deal. (Math students: See me later for an explanation.)

It happened once in the early days of Brookhaven's Duplicate Bridge Club, but only because a new deck had failed to be properly shuffled and then was improperly divided into four hands before being inserted into the duplicate board. Whether this was accidental or a fiendish practical joke has never been established, but in any event, it was in Board # 1 at a table where the old master, Charlie, was sitting South and one of his favorite partners, W.C., sitting North. Two esteemed matrons of the game were East and West, their names deliberately forgotten to protect the author.

Robert E. Jones

The hand came out as follows:

NORTH
S -
H - A Q J 10 9 8 7 6 5 4 3 2
D - A
C -

WEST
S -
H -
D - K Q J 10 9 8 7 6 5 4
C - K Q J

EAST
S - A K Q J 10 9 8 7 6 5 4 3 2
H -
D -
C -

SOUTH
S -
H - K
D - 3 2
C - A 10 9 8 7 6 5 4 3 2

South Deals Both Vulnerable

The Bidding

SOUTH	WEST	NORTH	EAST
Pass!	5 **D**	6 **H**	7 **S**
7NT!	Pass	Pass	Double(?)
Pass	Pass	Pass	

204

Mississippi Gumbo

Charlie's hand was the most nearly normal of the deal, and rather than pre-empt at four or five clubs, he simply passed.

The esteemed matron sitting West took several minutes to control her nervousness as she viewed the first ten-card suit she could ever remember holding. She counted and recounted the diamonds and wiped her glasses to make sure no hearts were mixed up therein. Then she confidently bid five diamonds, not exactly a reckless challenge with only the two missing aces as potential losers.

W.C. took a couple extra sips of coffee to clear his head and then went into a deep trance of intense concentration until steam began escaping from his ears. Finally, after rearranging his cards one more time, he bid six hearts. He later explained he didn't bid seven because of the possibility of an opening diamond lead being trumped! Since East would be leading to West, the diamond bidder, this reasoning will not go down in bridge annals as an example of astute logic. However, we can't fault him for not making the best bid while trying to control his blood pressure with such a monumental holding.

Finally, it came East's turn to bid. She had had to endure the interminable and agonizing bidding trances by South, West, and North and had hardly been able to keep her seat, squirming and fighting a desperate urge to run to the powder room. She could hardly wait to proudly bid her lifelong dream of SEVEN SPADES and enjoy coolly laying down the solid 13-card spade suit and claiming her grand slam. Her glare at North for his long delay had grown darker minute by minute, as her patience wore thin. When he had finally bid his six hearts and before it stopped echoing off the bare walls of the old Y-Hut building, she triumphantly and proudly announced her thoughtful bid of SEVEN SPADES! She exhaled, tried to conceal her glee, and eased back in her chair to savor the exquisite pleasure of the moment, nodding assuredly at her startled partner.

East's satisfaction turned into irritation as Charlie thoughtfully paused and mused before bidding. The additional delay further infuriated her. She wondered if he would be stupid enough to double. "Ha! Ha!...Wait! You don't suppose he's thinking about sacrificing at Seven No Trump? Oh, No!! If he does, I'll kill him. I'll double, and he'll be buried in penalty points! That'll teach him, the smart aleck!"

Charlie thought, "This is obviously an extremely freak hand. East has got to have all 13 spades, so she can never get the lead to cash a trick. West may very well be missing the Diamond ace since she bid only five - that puts the Diamond ace in W.C.'s hand along with an extremely long heart suit. With my heart king and club ace, we could take it all." (At least, that's how he explained it later.) "SEVEN NO TRUMP!" he trumpeted, and feigning boredom, looked at the ceiling and drummed his fingers.

Stunned, West and North, in their dazes, mumbled "pass," but East, in a fury, indignantly doubled, outraged that she should be denied the once in a lifetime pleasure of laying down a cold grand slam with 13 trumps. She glared at Charlie and nodded smugly at her partner, who was now nearly catatonic from excess adrenalin.

Mississippi Gumbo

It is not recorded whether West opened a Diamond or a Club, but it doesn't matter since the slam was unbeatable as long as South played the Ace of Hearts on the King at the second or third trick.

The post mortem was raucous and heated with everyone defending their bids. Charlie merely smiled and coolly lit another Camel. West inquired of East how she could double holding a dead hand when West, who would be choosing the opening lead, had declined to double. East's explanation is lost to history, but she covered up nicely by loudly calling for the director and claiming the hand was a fraud.

I don't remember if the hand stood or was thrown out by the director—it doesn't matter.

It was a hand to remember.

A CLOWN OR A WITCH?

My middle child, Jennifer, was always sweet and loving, as well as full of fun, and just mischievous enough to be normal.

She loved Halloween, and the costume to be worn was chosen only after days of careful thought and inner debate. Once, when she was about preschool age, she announced on Halloween afternoon that she wanted to be a witch. That was her adamant choice for the big night.

This created a problem for the household management for there was no witch costume in inventory, and management hoped to avoid the expense and trouble of finding and purchasing another Halloween attire at the last minute.

Her mother tried to divert Jennifer's desire to other possible outfits. "How about going as a pirate? We've got a great pirate suit your brother used to wear."

"I wanna be a witch."

"I know! How about being a GHOST! We can make you into a wonderful ghost with an old sheet with eyeholes! Wouldn't that be fun!"

"I wanna be a witch."

"How about that funny clown suit we've got?"

"I wanna be a witch," sniff, sniff.

"Here's Daddy, let's see what he thinks."

"So you want to be a witch?"

"Yes Sir."

"Oh, great, I tell you what—Ssh! (conspiratorially) You can be a witch—disguised as a clown!"

"I can?"

"Yes—No one will know you are really a witch unless you tell them. You can tell the secret to your best friends, but nobody else."

With this, she enthusiastically donned the clown suit and eagerly awaited trick or treating time as a genuine witch pretending to be a clown.

This diplomatic coup was probably my greatest achievement as a father.

Jennifer, in real life, eventually became a successful wife and mother, and she practices her chosen profession. Her disposition grows sweeter with every passing year, and now, this Halloween, she is really an angel disguised as a dentist.

THE SENATOR GOES TO NASHVILLE

The elegant Plantation Club was the top choice for snazzy nightlife in post-World War II Nashville, Tennessee. The nightspot saw many a celebrity, politician, entertainer, and tycoon enjoy its fine steaks, excellent drinks, and danceable music.

But one special night may stand out in the annals of the club.

The nattily attired "Senator" Matt Largent; Charles Emmette ("Fast Charlie") Brennan, his bodyguard and advisor for domestic affairs; and one, Bill ("The Judge") Peeler, his advisor for all other affairs, soaked up the atmosphere in the prestigious Plantation Club, one dizzy spring night in 1950.

Charlie has just slipped a buck to the Master of Ceremonies and confided in him that the elderly gentleman at his table was the esteemed senior senator from Florida, Senator Matt Largent.

After a drum roll, spot light, and the public address announcement of the presence of such a distinguished visitor, the table was besieged by eager political wanabees, gushing widows, and other interested onlookers. They offered free drinks and desired handshakes or a seat on the Senator's lap with a kiss on the cheek, depending upon the preference of the individual.

This was the climax of a night on the town by Charlie and his friend Bill Peeler who along with their chum and mascot, Matt Largent, had traveled the 32 miles to Nashville from Lebanon,

Tennessee, where Charlie and Peeler were attending Cumberland Law School.

Largent, a Lebanon character, was an ex-jockey who claimed to have ridden Jesse James' stallion in a horse race many years before on a nearby racetrack. Now he was retired from the strain of being an ex-jockey and lived alone in a dirt-floored shack a few miles out of town with his little fiest dog and his nearly blind old nag who provided his only means of transportation by pulling a rickety wagon to and from town.

Charlie had arrived in the unpolished rural East Tennessee town of Lebanon after his discharge from the Marines in 1946 to pursue training for the legal profession, a family tradition. Uncannily, he had quickly homed in on a spot known as "The Devil's Elbow," composed of a pool hall on the corner, flanked on one side by Joe Jordan's restaurant and on the other by the Brass Rail—a no frills beer dispensary, with a long bar and no chairs or tables. The proprietor had discovered, after much experience, that he could sell more beer per hour per square foot if customers were required to remain standing, rather than having them leisurely lounging in comfortable chairs and laying their heads on tables.

It was in the first few hours of Charlie's discovery of this charming establishment that he met Matt Largent. Brennan had noticed a scraggly horse-shaped animal with a wagon tied to a parking meter in front of the Brass Rail. And then a Popeye-type human being entered the warmth and gayety of the Brass Rail. The bewhiskered individual was dressed, uh—informally in ragged shirt, dirty overalls, and eggbeater styled hair. But in spite of his unimposing appearance, the regular customers warmly greeted him upon his entrance.

Striding proudly to the bar, he slapped down a check of some sort; and taking a stub pencil from the bartender in his fist, he scraped a fine "X" on the back of the check. Upon this, the bartender loudly announced, "OK, beer's on Matt," amid the cheers of the regulars.

Upon inquiry over this curious event, Charlie learned that every month when Matt got his county pauper's check, he wasted no time in taking it to the Brass Rail to set up everyone there with beer until it was exhausted. In return, all other days of the month, he was entitled to be set up with unlimited beer by the regular customers of the joint. It was an arrangement welcome to all - the owner, the regulars, and Matt.

Charlie and his law school buddies soon became strong supporters of Matt and enjoyed many an evening of philosophical and intellectual discussions of weighty matters of current interest while lifting a can of suds or two. They valued his opinion on many subjects as they regarded him as a man of the people, experienced in many areas of life. And besides, he had a ready means of transportation available to get them to and from school—the nag and wagon—which also came in handy for beer drinking hay rides, although curiously they were never able to get any girls to come along. Few of the students on the GI bill had automobiles in those first years following World War II.

Robert E. Jones

The big event at the Nashville nightclub came about as Charlie and Peeler planned how to celebrate the end of first semester exams. Making the trek to the bright lights and excitement of Nashville immediately came to mind—and then, to make it a memorable pilgrimage, they would take Matt along with them. However, this required (a) cleaning Matt thoroughly (a daunting challenge) and (b) clothing him suitably.

The (b) requirement was readily satisfied from the donation of a three-piece suit another friend had won in a crap game and with the loan of a Homburg hat and a smart cane. Requirement (a) was a little tougher; but finally with the offer of handsome tips and free beers later, a barber agreed to undertake the task of bathing, shampooing, shaving, and hair cutting the old gentleman. After his shampoo, Charlie and Peeler were astounded to discover that Largent's hair was almost white rather than the burnt umber it had always appeared.

Finally, the day arrived, and the "soon to be" senator and his entourage embarked on a Greyhound to Nashville. After enjoying good steaks, (Matt somehow managed to consume his with gusto, in spite of lacking lower teeth, having knocked his steak to the floor, and valiantly trying to properly use the unfamiliar knife and fork.) the trio set out for a tour of the nightlife of the city. Some events are best left to the reader's imagination, but eventually they found themselves the center of attention at the Plantation Club.

Their return to Lebanon in the wee hours after missing the last bus was accomplished by pooling all of their remaining funds and haggling a starving cab driver to make the trip back to Lebanon for about one-tenth the usual fare.

Thereafter, Matt was greatly respected in Lebanon and honored as the esteemed "Senator" Largent until his dying day.

MY FRIEND CHARLIE

My good friend Charlie Brennan died in August, 1997, in a tragic fire. I miss him.

From his Irish genes, he had both talents and faults, like most of us. One of his loves was music. Songs from Irish tenors could keep him enraptured for hours. When he got near an unguarded piano, he was apt to ripple out a melodic composition of his own, though he had never taken a lesson.

Poetry was also a love. He had composed numerous poems that he would recite on occasion. I insisted he put some down on paper. One was a short war poem, but all he could recall was the first verse:

> A raindrop falls
>   A flower blooms
> A man just died
>   Here in the gloom.
>
> Oh, up the hill
>   Brave men you must
> With rifle shot
>   And bayonet thrust.
>
> Defend your flag
>   Defend your home
> Die if you must
>   Here 'crost the foam.

Robert E. Jones

His greatest epic was about violent revenge of a victim of robbery:

THE STRANGER MAN

The stranger man came through the eerie night
His head all bloody as from a fight.
Murmurs and curses were his only sound,
But his song was heard throughout the town
'bout the dirty dog who clopped him down,
Took his purse and left him to drown.

Headed straight for Jake's all-night saloon
Long strides in time to a tonky tune
He made his way through the swinging door
His own red blood trailing 'cross the floor
Looking for that snake who clopped him down,
Took his purse and left him to drown.

His blood shot eyes searched the smoke filled air;
But the man, **his man** wasn't there.
Now at the bar he drank his fill
And cried at last, "I've come to kill,
To kill the man who clopped me down,
Took my purse and left me to drown."

"Who's seen a man a 'wearing black
Carryin' twin pearls to shoot you in the back."
Monk the Drunk hollered with a sneer,
"What the hell do you want here?"
The Stranger Man quickly called his hand
With one swift blow, he bruised his pan,
"I'm looking for the coward who clopped me down,
Took my purse and left me to drown."

Mississippi Gumbo

A sudden quick movement caught his eye
And all there knew one had to die
As stranger man fired from his left hip low
The fool that drew had been "Rough Neck Joe."
"That warn't him" the Stranger Man said,
"And I ain't gonna go till he's lying dead,
That dirty skunk that clopped me down,
Took my purse and left me to drown."

The back room door made barely a squeak
Then opened full, and there stood the sneak!
Backed by three friends, he shouted out,
"Try yourself now you stinking lout!"
All hearts stopped in a terror-filled hush
Behind bloody whiskers, there rose a blush
Though none could see through such a mess
But a quick sharp smile and one could guess
That here was the man who had clopped him down,
Took his purse and left him to drown.

The curtain was up for the final show;
All there knew that one had to go.
They waited, waited for the deadly test
Stranger Man faced one of the best.
For "Black Jack Jim" as all knew well
Had sent at least fifty straight to hell.
They knew he had clopped Stranger Man down,
Took his purse and left him to drown.

The lights flickered dim from lack of air,
As the two sweaty foes continued to glare.
Then Stranger Man offered a final toast
In a voice from the grave as that of a ghost,
"Here's to a cowardly black-hearted freak
A dirty stinking motherless sneak
Who with a laugh will clop you down,
Take your purse and leave you to drown."

> To this cold-hearted toast only Stranger Man drank
> As all in the bar cowered and shrank.
> At last, Black Jack Jim turned and spoke,
> "Draw when you please," cut through the smoke.
> Then thunderous sounds and flashes of red
> Shattered the night and delivered the dead.
> The echoes died of four rounds spent
> From the right hip low of the Stranger Gent,
> And Black Jack Jim and the three at his back
> All lay twitching in a big fat stack.
> "Never again will he clop me down,
> Steal my purse and leave me to drown."
>
> The Stranger Man left through the eerie night
> With his head all bloody as from a fight.
> Murmurs and curses were his only sound;
> But his song had been heard throughout the town;
> And quickly the story spread through the fog
> How the Stranger Man handled the stinkin' dog
> Who with a sneer had clopped him down,
> Stole his purse and left him to drown.

Charlie was sometimes a lonely and pensive fellow. At his graveside service, few, if any, other mourners noticed the many scattered birdseeds around the gravesite, where Charlie had sat at his family plot watching the birds and throwing them seeds.

Known as "Slick Dog," Charlie had many wild escapades in his days at Cumberland Law School after he got out of the Marine Corps in the late 40's. He had a sharp intellect and was one of the main stays at the Brookhaven Duplicate Bridge Club for many years.

Charlie was an eternal optimist. No matter how broke he was, he would always look forward for something good that he was sure would happen soon, although it rarely ever happened.

Mississippi Gumbo

In the predawn darkness the other day retrieving my morning paper, I was struck by the brightness of Venus in the Eastern sky and was reminded of the epitaph Charlie had long requested, "Even upon the darkest night, I can always see a star."

JUDGMENT DAY

A Ten-Minute Play

SET: COURTROOM

Bailiff: **Hear Ye Hear Ye—The 23rd District Court of Heaven is now in session—The Honorable Judge Samuel Smathers appointed by God to hear issues of disposition of souls.**

Bailiff: **The next case your honor, is that of Heinreich Gorman and Sarah Grubman. Their cases have been consolidated because of the intertwining of their lives and their deaths.**

Judge: **Very well. Are they present?**

Bailiff: **Yes your honor** - (to subjects) **Please stand and face the bench.**

(Gorman and Grubman face the bench)

Heavenly Advocate: **Your Honor—The complete life reviews have been completed and viewed by the angel jury BUT the jury could not reach a unanimous decision and defers to your judgment. A summary of their lives is as follows:**

Robert E. Jones

Heinreich Gorman was born in Munich, Germany in 1923 to devout Christian protestant parents. He accepted Christ as his savior at age 12 and was a regular church attendant until about age 15. At that time, he joined the Nazi Youth Corps. He was trained in Nazi ideology and was urged and intimidated to withdraw from all religious activities. His uncle was an officer in the German SS and got him admitted into the elite SS Corp at 19 years of age when the war was raging. However, since his aptitude and IQ did not measure up to their requirements, he was assigned to the concentration camp guard service. He married a young Christian girl and they had two little daughters. He was placed in charge of a small death camp in Poland. His main duties were supervising the orderly extermination of the Jews in the camp and selecting the ones to be killed next. He personally shot to death many of the prisoners by firing his luger into their heads and then having their bodies put into the gas chamber. He says the ones he shot were done so out of mercy so their death would be instantaneous without suffering. He maintained that he was forced to do these unthinkable things by his superiors and that he would have been shot if he refused and his family would have been persecuted and impoverished. He claims he accepted Christ at an early age and continued throughout his life to be a secret Christian to the extent that he was permitted by his circumstances. He claims he prayed for his victims and prayed for their souls.

Your honor, his story has been verified and the heavenly prayer records confirm his claims of praying for his victims. Since he fulfilled the scriptural requirements for salvation, we submit that he should be admitted to the life everlasting as promised in the scripture, although it is confessed that it should be at the primary or lowest level of the kingdom.

Judge: Does the Devil's advocate have anything to submit?

Damon, The Devil's Advocate: Your Honor I admire the Heavenly Advocate for his unique ability to maintain his composure and a straight face when making such a preposterous plea in this matter. Do you think there is a place in your heaven that is low enough to accept a vicious, cold-blooded murderer of men, women and little children without a protest to his superiors or any heroic efforts to withhold his deadly hand. His plea of putting a bullet through their heads as an act of mercy is audaciously brazen and shatters his fragile credibility. Mercy Indeed!

Listen your honor, we need men like this in our little community. He'll do well in Hell. How could it even be contemplated that he be admitted to the company of angels and saints. You'll be putting us out of business. Holy Mackerel, Have mercy on us!

Judge: This case has been consolidated with another—that of Sarah Grubman. Before making any decision on Gorman, I believe we should hear the Grubman matter first.

<u>Heavenly Advocate</u>: **Yes, Your Honor.**

Sarah Grubman was born in Krakow, Poland in 1917 to devout Jewish parents and had her bas Mitzvah in 1930, married a Jewish boy in 1936, had two children before they were all arrested and put in the concentration camp on October 10, 1942. That was the last she saw of her husband. Her children were taken from her shortly thereafter and by the time of her death in 1945, she never knew what happened to any of them. In the camp she did menial work, including cleaning the bathroom and offices of the German commandment, Major Heinrich Gorman. In doing this work, she at times was spoken to by the Major, and they became acquainted. He told her about his family and inquired about her background and her family and her religion. He asked her if she knew about Jesus Christ. She told him she knew of Jesus through her studies and thought he was a prophet and a man of great wisdom, love and compassion, but she had been taught that the messiah had not yet come and that Jesus was not he. As the number of the prisoners was dwindling due to the regular executions, Major Gorman, she believed, deliberately avoided putting her name on the execution list. But finally when the war was about lost and the Russians were approaching the area, the Camp got orders to speed up the executions and to finish them all off within a week. Then an SS Colonel came to the camp and adamantly demanded that Major Gorman finish the job within 48 hours. There were about 200 prisoners remaining. The Colonel told Major Gorman that if he didn't get it done he would

Mississippi Gumbo

be sent to join the units trying to stop the Russian onslaught. The Colonel also told Major Gorman that he and Gorman's uncle were trying to arrange for Gorman's family to be moved to a place of safety in Austria, but that Gorman must complete his task first.

Later the major called for Sarah Gruber to come to his office.

After a long pause, he told her he had been praying for her, he wept and asked her to look out of the window at the camp yard. Sarah knew what he was about to do. She told him she understood what he had to do and she forgave him and would pray for him. It was then that he put a bullet through her head.

Judge: **Sarah Gruber never accepted Jesus as the Son of God?**

Heavenly Advocate: **No your honor, but even though He said on earth that "no one comes to the father except by me", He still reigns here and we ask that her case be submitted directly to Him for a decision.**

Judge: **What do you have to say Damon?**

Devil's Advocate: **Listen, you guys always preach that the gospel is the gospel. How can anyone believe what you say if you start letting anybody, just because they were good people into this kingdom. We have a lot of "good people" in our bailiwick if she didn't meet the scriptural requirements she's mine, right? We'll be good to her, don't worry.**

Judge: I'd like to ask the candidates a couple of questions.

Gorman, did you truly accept Christ as your savior as a young man?

Gorman: Yes your honor.

Judge: Then how could you commit such cruel, evil, heinous crimes that you did?

Gorman: I don't deserve any mercy your honor. The devil's advocate is right. I deserve to go to his kingdom but I want you to know I hated myself for doing what I did. I am and was so ashamed for lacking the courage to refuse my orders—I was a pitiful coward—I was afraid for my dear family and as long as they can be admitted to your Kingdom, I will willingly go with Damon to the depths of hell. But please have mercy on Sarah Gruber. She was not taught about Christ. She didn't have a chance to accept. She is a beautiful pure innocent soul. Please I beg of you, send me to Hell but spare her.

Judge: That will be all, Heinreich Gorman.

Mrs. Gruber, what do you say?

Sarah Gruber: Your honor, poor Heinreich Gorman, he couldn't help himself. He was taught to obey orders absolutely without question. He just was not born with courage—and he really had no choice in what he did. Please have mercy on him. I have forgiven him and please have mercy on him.

Judge: This is a trying case—I do not feel that I can make the decision on either of your cases.

Therefore, I am sending your cases up to the Son for his personal attention.

NEXT CASE!

Made in the USA
Columbia, SC
27 July 2018